# The Knock Airport Mystery

VINCENT MCDONNELL is from County Mayo and now
lives near Newmarket, County Cork. In 1989 he won
the GPA First Fiction Award, after being recommended
by Graham Greene, and has since had seven novels for
children published and two for adults. Many of his
short stories have also been published and he has won
numerous other prizes as well as being shortlisted for
the RAI awards. He has been writer in residence at a
variety of locations and has given workshops
and readings all over Ireland.

Other children's titles by the same author

FOR MY MOTHER

# The Knock Airport Mystery

## Vincent McDonnell

The Collins Press

Published in 2005 by
The Collins Press
West Link Park
Doughcloyne
Wilton
Cork

© Vincent McDonnell 2005
© Illustrations Deirdre O'Neill 2005

First published in 1993 by Poolbeg Press

Vincent McDonnell has asserted his moral right to be identified
as author of this work.

A Cataloguing-In-Publication data record for this book is available from the British Library

ISBN: 1-903464-87-0

*Typesetting:* The Collins Press

*Font:* Hoefler Text, 14 point

*Cover design:* Deirdre O'Neill

Printed in Ireland by Colour Books Ltd

# IN THE PRISON

Pug Banzinni restlessly paced his prison cell. Up and down he marched, like a sentry on duty. Now and then he glanced up at the barred window high above his head and yearned for freedom. Bright shafts of summer sunshine pierced the gloom and illuminated the motes of dust which swirled in the air. But Pug Banzinni hardly noticed this. His mind was solely occupied with thoughts of escape.

For months this cell had been his whole world. He had only left it when he appeared in court. Each time his lawyer had assured him he would soon be free and Banzinni had trusted him. But his hopes had been dashed when a judge told him he would soon be sent back to America.

For years Pug Banzinni had been the most feared criminal in America. He had ruled his gang of thugs with an iron fist, crushing anyone who dared oppose him. Before he became a criminal he had been a boxer. As a result he had lost his front teeth, and his nose had been squashed as flat as a mushroom. It was this squashed nose that had earned him the nickname Pug.

The American police did everything in their power to catch him but he was too clever for them. One day though he made a mistake. Another gang robbed a bank that Pug Banzinni himself was planning to rob. When he heard this he became enraged and ordered his henchmen to bring the leader of this other gang to him for punishment.

The leader was brought to Banzinni's hideout and pleaded with him not to be punished. But Banzinni ignored his pleas. Instead he beat the man with his fists and ordered that he be given the dreaded concrete sock treatment.

Two large buckets of concrete were mixed and the man was forced to place one foot in each bucket. When the concrete had set, Pug ordered his henchmen to throw the unfortunate victim out into the street.

The man managed to hobble back to his own hideout. There, his right-hand man took a hammer and chisel and slowly chipped away the concrete. It was a long, painful task. By the time he was finished, his boss' feet were black and blue. Both big toes and one of his little toes were broken.

He was in terrible pain and wanted revenge. So he went to the police and told them what had happened. Now the police had a reason to arrest Pug Banzinni. They knew that once he was locked up others he had beaten and robbed would come forward to testify against him in court. And when they did, Banzinni would be sent to prison for the rest of his life.

The police raced towards Pug's hideout to arrest him. But Banzinni had been tipped off and escaped. He was now a wanted man and knew that every policeman in America would be looking for him. His only hope lay in leaving the country. Banzinni kept a false passport for just such an emergency and now he ordered his driver to take him to Kennedy Airport.

At the airport Banzinni discovered that a flight was about to take off for Ireland. There was one vacant seat on board. Pug knew it was his last chance of escape and he bought a ticket under a false name. A few minutes later he was on board and within an hour was flying high above the Atlantic.

When the police reached Banzinni's hideout they discovered he had escaped.

'He'll try and leave the country,' Captain Cooper, who

was in charge of the policemen, said. 'We must stop him.'

With sirens blaring they raced through the streets of New York to Kennedy Airport. There they checked if passenger Banzinni had booked onto any flight. But no one of that name had done so.

'He must have used a false passport,' Captain Cooper said. 'We'll show his photograph instead and see if anyone recognises him.'

They found an official who remembered Banzinni from the photograph.

'That's Mr Jones,' the official said. 'I remember him because he had a pug-nose and his front teeth were missing. He was in a terrible hurry. He caught a flight to Ireland.'

Captain Cooper did not hesitate. He rushed to the nearest telephone and within minutes was speaking to the authorities in Ireland.

Hours later, when the aircraft landed in Ireland, Pug Banzinni, to his surprise and horror, was arrested by the gardai. He made a desperate attempt to escape but three gardai overpowered him. He was handcuffed and taken away. The next day he appeared in court and the judge sent him to prison while he decided what should be done with him.

For months Pug had languished in prison, awaiting

his fate. Now the judge had decided to send him back to America to stand trial. Pug knew his only hope lay in escaping from prison.

At the moment his trusted henchmen were in Ireland and were planning to free him. He had ordered them to do so under the threat of the concrete sock treatment if they didn't. Deep in thought as he pondered how they might free him, Banzinni was now disturbed by a key turning in the lock of his cell door.

'You've got a visitor,' a warder said, opening the door. 'You must come with me.'

Banzinni followed the warder, thinking this was part of an escape plan. But the warder took him to a room where his right-hand man, Scarface Moran, was waiting for him.

Moran was as thin as a flagpole. His long nose had been broken in many fights and was like the knurled root of a tree. On his right cheek was the deep knife scar which had given him his nickname.

Banzinni and Moran exchanged greetings until the warder was out of earshot. Then Banzinni grabbed Moran's arm and dug his nails deep into the flesh.

'When are you gonna get me out of here?' he demanded in his tough-guy, American accent.

'Ouch, Boss,' Moran said. 'You're hurting me.'

'Hurting you!' Banzinni growled between his teeth. 'I'll tear your arm off and beat you over the head with it. Now answer my question and be quick about it. I don't want to spend another day in here.'

'You'll have to, Boss,' Moran said.

'Have to?' Banzinni tightened his grip. He was immensely strong and Moran thought his arm would be crushed.

'Only for a few more days,' Moran whimpered. 'I've got a plan to free you. Let me tell you all about it.'

'OK,' Banzinni said. 'Talk.'

'We ... we couldn't free you from here,' Moran said. 'It's too risky and dangerous.'

'You telling me you're scared?' Banzinni demanded.

'No, Boss. I'm not scared. But the prison is well protected. There's a high wall all around the outside. It's topped with barbed wire and there are guards with dogs patrolling it. It would be very difficult to escape. Anyway, we don't have time to plan it all properly.'

'You don't have time,' repeated Banzinni. 'Whadya mean by that?' In his confusion he released Moran's arm.

'You're to be sent back to America on Friday,' Moran said. 'You'll be handed over to two detectives from New York and put on board a jumbo jet bound for Kennedy Airport.'

Banzinni reacted angrily and Moran edged away from

him. He had known his boss for many years and was aware he lashed out with his iron-hard fists when angry.

'I'll be put in prison there,' Banzinni wailed. 'They'll lock me up forever. I'll never get to rob another bank.'

'But I'm going to free you,' Moran interrupted.

'Free me?' Banzinni asked. 'You're not going to give me a parachute and suggest that I jump from the aircraft?'

'Oh, you can be so funny, Boss,' Moran giggled.

'Funny!' Banzinni hissed. 'I'll give you funny. Now tell me how you're gonna rescue me from an aeroplane flying at 30,000 feet up in the clouds? Especially as you can't free me from a prison which as you can see has not even left the ground.'

'Sshh,' Moran warned. 'Or the warder'll hear us.' He had noticed that the warder was edging closer to try to overhear their conversation.

'OK,' Banzinni whispered, getting his anger under control. 'Tell me about this plan of yours.'

Moran looked around him. He saw that the warder was still trying to listen so he drew Banzinni further away before outlining his plan. The warder craned his head but could only hear snatches of the conversation. He heard a helicopter being mentioned and something about a decoy. But it didn't make sense. Then Moran spoke of a hearse and a coffin and a ship at sea. Maybe they had known a sailor who had been buried at sea, the warder thought. Then he heard Moran mention Knock Airport in County Mayo. At this point the warder began to think of his dinner.

When Moran finished speaking there was silence. He was worried about Pug's reaction and cringed in case he should lash out with his fists. But instead Banzinni had a big grin on his face which showed his missing front teeth.

'It's brilliant,' he said. 'It's the best plan I've ever heard.'

Moran was pleased with the praise. He knew he was in for a large bonus once Banzinni was free. And that meant that by Friday evening he would be rich.

Banzinni gripped Moran's arm and asked him a number of questions about the plan. But Moran was able to answer every one of them. An hour later, when Moran left the prison, Pug Banzinni was happy. He knew that in another few days he would be a free man again.

# 2

## AT KNOCK AIRPORT

Kevin Dolan was bored. It seemed ages since he had arrived at Knock Airport with his father, elder brother David and sister Cathy. He wished the aeroplane bringing his cousin Alan from England would arrive soon and they could go home.

Aeroplanes held no interest for Kevin. All they did was fly and make a lot of noise. They were just like birds. But that wasn't quite right, of course. Birds could build nests and lay eggs and drop a runny, smelly whoopsy on your head.

Now, tractors were interesting. Kevin loved them, with their smells of diesel and exhaust fumes. They could operate all sorts of fascinating farm machinery like hay-mowers and hay-turners and best of all, hay-balers.

But there was an even more fascinating machine than the tractor or hay-baler. This was the mechanical digger, just like the one parked by the airport fence. Kevin had spotted it earlier and was anxious to see it close up. If only he could slip quietly away without anyone noticing.

Just then Cathy yelled. She had been scanning the sky for sight of the aeroplane and at that moment had seen it out to the west. It was swinging about in a giant arc as it made its final approach to the airport.

'There it is!' she exclaimed, pointing with her finger.

David swung his head around, his father's binoculars clamped to his eyes.

'I can hear it,' he said, 'but I can't see it.' Then he too caught sight of the aeroplane, as yet little more than a speck in the distance. 'I can see it now,' he said, clearly excited.

Kevin too could see the aeroplane, by now the size of a seagull. But he still preferred to look at the mechanical digger.

'It'll soon be landing,' Thomas Dolan said. 'We'll go into the arrivals hall and wait for your cousin there.'

'Can't we stay here, Dad?' Cathy asked. 'We could wave to Alan as the plane lands.'

'OK,' her father agreed. 'But when it lands you must

come into the arrivals hall.' With that, Mister Dolan walked off towards the terminal building.

David and Cathy were bubbling with excitement at the prospect of being reunited with their cousin, who came to visit them each summer. But Kevin wasn't that excited. Alan was four years older than Kevin and he was interested only in playing with David. Sometimes they did allow Kevin to play football with them but that wasn't very often.

Cathy and David were whispering excitedly together as they watched the aeroplane approach.

'I'm bored,' Kevin said to Cathy. 'Can I go and look at the digger?'

'Oh, I suppose you can,' Cathy said. 'But don't go too far.'

'I won't,' Kevin promised and, as fast as his legs could carry him, he raced across the car park to the yellow JCB. The driver had gone for his lunch and had left the cab door open. Kevin furtively looked around to make sure no one was watching. Then, in a flash, he climbed up into the cab.

Kevin had never been in a JCB before and he found himself so high up in the air that he thought he would become dizzy. He felt he was as high in the air as the aeroplane coming in to land. But he was sure the aeroplane didn't have as many interesting levers as the JCB. Nor did it have as big a steering wheel. David had told him yesterday that aeroplanes didn't have steering wheels, but Kevin didn't believe that.

He sat in the driver's seat and pretended to operate the machine. He pursed his lips and blew out air, making a noise like an engine. With one hand on the steering wheel, he operated the various levers with the other.

He was so engrossed in what he was doing that he took no notice of the limousine which drove into the car park and stopped beside the machine. It wasn't until he heard the slam of the closing doors that he glanced out. Two men had got out of the black limousine, one of them carrying a briefcase.

Kevin realised that if he were caught in the JCB he might get into trouble. Quickly he slipped down from the seat, intending to jump from the cab and run. But he was too late. The two men were already walking towards him. They came right up to the open door, blocking his escape route. Kevin crouched on the floor and held his breath.

The men stood with their backs to the open door.

'Well, whatdya think, Tiny?' the man with the brief-case said. He had an American accent, a bit like Kevin's Aunt Mary who had come to visit them from New York last summer.

'Seems perfect, Slim,' Tiny answered. He too had an American accent.

Despite his fear, Kevin nearly burst out laughing. The man called Tiny was over six feet tall and must have weighed sixteen stone. He wore a black hat and when he moved, Kevin could see muscles rippling beneath the material of his black suit.

In contrast, the man called Slim was short and fat. He was only a few inches over five feet yet weighed as much as his companion. He had a large, shiny, bald head and the flesh of his neck was corrugated. He seemed to be about to burst out of his suit like an over-ripe plum.

'Looks like it was made for us,' Slim said. 'It's a fair distance to the nearest cop shop – they call them Garda stations here – and we'll be long gone before they arrive on the scene. I'd say Pug himself couldn't be more pleased if he saw it.'

'He'll see it on Friday,' Tiny said, 'if our plan to free him is a success.'

'It had better be a success,' Slim said. 'Otherwise Pug'll give us the concrete sock treatment.'

'Mister Banzinni will have you flayed alive as well if he hears you using that name,' Tiny warned. 'You know he hates it. And he won't be in a terribly good mood after spending so long in prison.'

'I'll be careful,' Slim said. 'I don't want no trouble. I just want to see the Boss free again. Then maybe we can go back to robbing banks. I've been so bored having nothing to do.'

At that moment the aeroplane approached the end of the runway and the roar of the engines was deafening. The two men became silent and watched the aeroplane as it touched down with a squeal of tyres and a puff of smoke.

Kevin was uncomfortable. He was squashed tight against the edge of the seat and the metal base was pressing against his ribs. It hurt and he wanted to ease his position but was frightened to do so. He realised the men were criminals and were planning a crime. He knew that if they saw him they would know he had overheard them. They wouldn't be able to let him go in case he told the gardai about them. Instead they would have to take him away with them. He would be locked up and given only bread and water to eat and drink. They wouldn't let him go until Friday when this Pug Banzinni, whoever he was, would be freed from prison.

He wished the men would go away. He wished he'd never left David and Cathy. He wished he had never been interested in diggers. In fact, if he got out of here safely, he would never go near a digger again.

The mighty roar as the jet engines went into reverse

thrust to slow the aeroplane died away and there was a more subdued roar as it taxied back to the terminal building.

'I think,' Slim said, now that he could be heard again, 'that we can let Moran know this place is perfect. We're lucky the runway can take a jumbo jet. Of course, there will be no problem with the helicopter. That's the really brilliant part of the plan. Moran is a genius to think of using a decoy. The police won't know where to look.'

'Our part of the plan is easy,' Tiny said. 'Moran has the difficult part. Do you think he'll be able to make Captain Mulligan do what he wants?'

'He told me that he's got it all worked out,' Slim said. 'He's going to pretend he's making a film just like us.' At this the two thugs laughed.

'We've just gotta make certain that we don't let him down,' Tiny added. 'We must have the hearse with the coffin ready on Friday afternoon and make sure everything goes to plan.'

'Then we've nothing to worry about,' Tiny said. 'So I think I'll have a large cigar to celebrate.'

He lit a fat cigar and Kevin crinkled his nose in distaste. Smoking was such a dirty habit. Now, to Kevin's horror, the smoke began to drift into the cab. It smelt horrible, like burning rubbish. His eyes watered and the smoke went up his nose and tickled the back of his throat.

He tried his best not to cough. But his effort only made him splutter. When he did cough, he couldn't stop. Through eyes half-blinded with tears, he saw the two men swing around towards him. Two angry and threatening pairs of eyes stared at him.

'What have we here?' Slim demanded. 'What are you doin', boy?'

Kevin tried to speak but was too frightened to do so. He couldn't get his tongue around the words.

'He's heard everything,' Tiny said. 'We can't let him go.'

'Please, sir!' Kevin pleaded, when he eventually found his voice. 'I ... I didn't hear anything.'

'He's just a boy,' Slim said. 'Maybe he didn't hear anything.'

'We can't take a chance,' Tiny warned. 'I'll cut out his tongue. Then he won't be able to tell anyone anything.'

'Oh, don't cut out my tongue,' Kevin wailed. 'Please don't.' If they cut out his tongue he would never be able to lick an ice-cream again.

'Shut up, boy,' Tiny growled, 'and let's see this tongue of yours.' He threw his cigar on the ground and squashed it with his shoe. Then his hand, which seemed enormous, reached into the cab to grab Kevin.

'Kevin? Kevin? Where are you?' It was Cathy's voice. Kevin was never more glad to hear it in his life.

'What's that?' Tiny withdrew his hand and swung around.

'Some girl,' Slim warned. 'She's comin' this way.'

Kevin saw his chance. He leapt up, banging his head on the steering wheel. But he took no notice of the pain.

'Cathy,' he called, jumping down from the cab and scampering across to her.

'There you are,' Cathy said. 'David and I have been waiting for you.'

'I was looking at the digger,' Kevin said. 'Then I heard those men planning to free some criminal. They were going to cut out my tongue.'

'You shouldn't tell fibs,' Cathy said. 'It's not nice.'

'But it's true,' Kevin protested. 'I heard them. He's Slim and he's Tiny and they're going to free this man called Pug Banzinni.'

'Oh Kevin, you fibber,' Cathy laughed. 'You can't go calling people names. Why, those gentlemen are ...' She seemed lost for words. 'I must apologise for my brother's behaviour,' Cathy said to Tiny and Slim. 'He isn't usually rude.'

'It's OK,' Slim said. 'We're from Hollywood and we're gonna be making a film here. Say, you're not an actress, are you? You're kinda pretty.'

'Me?' Cathy said. 'Oh, no. I mean, yes. I ... I was in the school play.'

'I thought so,' Slim said. 'You look like a movie star. We might have a part for you. Mind you, it's all kinda secret ...'

'Oh, I won't breathe a word,' Cathy said. 'And I'll make sure Kevin doesn't say a word either.'

'That's real fine,' Slim said. 'We'll be in touch about the film. Have a nice day now.' Both men turned away, walked to their limousine and drove off.

'Come on,' Cathy said to Kevin. 'Dad'll be looking for us.'

'They're not telling the truth,' Kevin protested. 'They are criminals. They're planning to free Pug Banzinni. He must be a criminal too because he's in prison. They said they could rob banks again when he was free.'

'They're making a film,' Cathy said. 'Didn't they just say so?'

'It's not true,' Kevin said. 'They're only pretending about the film. I'm going to tell Dad about them.'

'Oh no, you're not,' Cathy insisted. 'I promised that we wouldn't tell anyone about the film. So you keep quiet, otherwise I'll tell Dad about you. And you know what'll happen then. Now promise.'

'I promise,' Kevin said reluctantly. He knew when it was pointless to argue. Resigned to doing nothing, he followed his sister into the terminal building.

# 3

## KEVIN HEARS THE NEWS

As Cathy and Kevin entered the terminal building they saw Alan coming through the door marked 'Arrivals'.

'There's Alan,' Cathy cried, as she ran towards him. For the next few moments the Dolan family were caught up in the excitement of greeting their tall, fair-haired cousin. David was anxious to tell Alan of all the great things he had planned for both of them. 'There's fishing,' he said. 'And football and cycling and ...'

'... the turf,' his father laughed. 'I'm expecting you to help me with it. It has to be taken out to the roadside by pony and cart. So you can put that on your agenda of adventures.'

'Well, when we finish the turf, then we'll go cycling,'

David said to Alan. 'My friend Martin has loaned you his mountain bike. It's got fifteen gears and will climb anything.'

'Great!' Alan exclaimed. 'I love cycling.'

'Can I come with you?' Kevin asked.

'We'll see,' David said, and Kevin had to be satisfied with that.

They emerged into the sunshine and made their way to where Thomas Dolan had parked his jeep. As they left the car park Kevin took a last look at the JCB. He shuddered at the thought of what the two Americans might have done to him. He had been lucky Tiny hadn't cut out his tongue. If Cathy hadn't come along, he might have done just that.

Kevin still didn't believe what Slim had said about making a film. They really were criminals intent on freeing Pug Banzinni. But Kevin had never heard of such a man. He would have liked to ask his father who Pug Banzinni was. But his father would want to hear the whole story. And when he learned that Kevin had gone off on his own, he would be angry. So Kevin decided it might be best to keep the matter to himself.

They travelled along the road that ran parallel to the runway. A chain link fence prevented anyone from going on to airport property. There were a number of gates in the fence which gave access to the runway. Now, as they approached one of the gates, Kevin saw the Americans' limousine parked by the roadside. Slim and Tiny stood by the gate looking towards the runway. Tiny was smoking one of his fat cigars.

Kevin slid down in the seat until only his hair and eyes were visible above the edge of the window. He was frightened that if Slim or Tiny saw him they would write down the registration number of the jeep and find out where he lived. Then they would come to his house in the dead of night. They would creep into his darkened bedroom and cut out his tongue and he would bleed all over his mother's white sheets.

But despite his fear, Kevin nudged Cathy.

'There's those criminals,' he whispered, not taking his eyes off the two men as the jeep passed.

'Criminals? Did 1 hear you say criminals?' Kevin's whisper had been louder than he intended and David heard him.

'What criminals? Where are they?' David looked excitedly about him.

'There,' Kevin said, forgetting for the moment that he was likely to get into trouble. 'Those ... Ouch!' He gasped for breath as Cathy's elbow nudged him firmly in the ribs.

'Kevin is playing at being a detective,' Cathy said. 'He's pretending that everyone he sees is a criminal. I don't think that's very nice. He promised me only today that he wouldn't do things like that any more, didn't you, Kevin?' Cathy nudged him again with her elbow.

Kevin nodded, still clutching his ribs. He looked at Cathy and saw a threatening frown on her face. Furtively he glanced over his shoulder but the brow of the hill had taken the Americans and their limousine from view. Kevin hoped he would never see them again.

They reached home without further mishap and found Mary Dolan waiting for them. She was delighted to see Alan and had a warm welcome for him. Lunch was ready and they sat down to roast lamb, boiled potatoes, carrots and parsnips. Afterwards there was jelly and ice-cream and glasses of cool lemonade.

Alan had presents for everyone. There was perfume for Mary Dolan and a silk tie for Thomas. He brought David a set of walkie-talkies and a Walkman cd player for Cathy. Kevin got a remote control racing car.

Alan showed them a pocket voice recorder he had brought with him.

'I'm a reporter on the school magazine,' he said. 'I use the recorder to do interviews. I'm going to interview you all and write an article for the magazine about life on a farm.'

'Farm life means a lot of hard work,' Thomas Dolan laughed. 'I can tell you all about that.'

'Great,' Alan enthused. 'That's just what I want.'

They were all anxious to try out their presents and Thomas Dolan said they could have the afternoon to themselves. Alan and David went off to test the walkie-talkies while Cathy went to visit a friend. She set off with her favourite cd playing. Kevin took his racing car out to the yard. Here his father marked out a racing circuit with chalk and Kevin spent the afternoon pretending to be a champion racing driver.

At six o'clock Kevin was called for his tea. When he entered the kitchen the others were already seated at the table. Mary Dolan had prepared a salad. There was cold chicken and ham and hard-boiled eggs and lettuce and tomatoes and spring onions and blood-red beetroot. After tea Thomas Dolan excused himself and went into the living room to watch the weather forecast on the television.

Some minutes later Kevin joined his father and asked if he would mark out a longer racing track. 'I will indeed,' his father said. 'As soon as I've seen the weather forecast. It'll be on after the news headlines.'

Kevin found the news boring. He turned away from the television to look out the window at the flowering cherry, the petals of which had blanketed the lawn in June like pink snow. Just then he heard the newsreader mention the name Banzinni.

Immediately Kevin swung back to the television, interested now in what the newsreader had to say.

'It was announced this morning,' the newsreader said, 'that a judge has decided to send the American criminal, Pug Banzinni, back to New York. There he will stand trial for a great number of offences. A spokesman said that Mr Banzinni will be flown to New York this coming Friday afternoon.'

Kevin could hardly believe what he had heard. There really was a man named Pug Banzinni! And he was a criminal. It was this man that the two Americans had been talking about. They were planning to free him from prison. They had lied when they said they were making a film.

'Well then, Kevin,' Thomas Dolan said. 'Are you ready?'

'Ready?' Kevin was still deep in thought about the Americans and Pug Banzinni and the plan to free him from prison.

'To mark out the racing track,' his father laughed.

'Oh yes, Dad,' Kevin said.

He followed his father outside and watched as he marked out a track on the concrete. 'There you are,' his father said. 'Now, I must go off and bring the cows in for milking.'

'Thanks, Dad,' Kevin said. He picked up his racing car

and placed it on the new track. But he didn't race it any more. Instead he thought of the two Americans who were planning to free Pug Banzinni. What was he going to do about that? At the moment he was the only one who knew what they were planning. He was the only one who could stop them. But how could he do that? He knew they were cruel and heartless men. He would be in grave danger if he tried to thwart their plan. Yet despite that, he would have to do something to try and stop them.

He decided he would need help. But Cathy had already shown she was not going to be of any help. So there was no point asking her. If he told his father then he would get into trouble. The only people he could turn to were David and Alan. They would want to help. After all, they would be interested in adventure.

Kevin took his racing car inside and left it in his room. Then he went in search of David and Alan. If they were going to stop the Americans from freeing Pug Banzinni then there was little time to lose. Today was Monday. That meant that they only had four days in which to act.

# 4

## SEEKING MORE PROOF

Kevin found David and Alan in the summerhouse in a corner of the orchard. Originally it had been an old wooden shed which Thomas Dolan had converted. He had installed two windows so it was bright and sunny, and there were benches around the walls. The summerhouse contained a cd player and cds and a selection of books. Here, one could escape for a little while and listen to music or read in peace.

David and Alan were listening to a cd and didn't want to be disturbed. But Kevin's persistence paid off and David switched off the cd player.

Kevin told them what had happened at the airport and what he had just heard on the news.

'You're fibbing,' David said. 'I don't believe a word of it.'

'But it's true!' Kevin was upset at not being believed. He was trying to prevent a dangerous criminal from escaping, and no one would believe him or help him. 'I saw the men,' he said. 'They're called Slim and Tiny. They're going to free Pug Banzinni. They were going to cut out my tongue.'

David and Alan laughed. 'You know what you are?' David said. 'You're a pug-nose yourself. Anyway you are fibbing. Cathy said you were pretending to be a detective. So there.'

'I'm not,' Kevin insisted. 'She only said that because those men told her they were making a film and they promised her a part if she didn't tell anyone about it.'

'Now you really are fibbing,' David said. 'If Dad finds out, you'll be in trouble. You know how he hates lies.'

'They are not lies,' Kevin pleaded. 'Oh, why don't you believe me? You believe me, don't you, Alan?'

'I don't know,' Alan said. 'It sounds fishy to me.'

'There you are,' David said. 'Alan thinks it's all a right cod. Do you get it? Fishy ... all a right cod.' The two boys roared with laughter.

This upset Kevin even more. No one would believe him. He turned away and through the window saw his father driving the cows into the milking parlour.

'There's Dad,' Kevin said. 'Ask him. He'll tell you about Pug Banzinni.' Kevin caught David by the arm and tried to drag him outside.

'Oh, all right,' David said. 'But if you've been fibbing,' he added threateningly, 'I'll cut out your tongue myself.'

The three ran across the orchard to the yard where Thomas Dolan was shooing the last cow into the parlour.

'Dad,' David called. 'Can we ask you something?'

'What is it?' Thomas Dolan asked.

'Do you know anyone called Pug?' David asked.

At this, Thomas Dolan's face became stern and a spark of anger flashed in his eyes. 'I hope you've not been making fun of anyone,' he threatened. 'Haven't I warned you often enough about nicknames?'

'It's not me,' David said quickly. 'It's Kevin. He was just telling us about someone called Pug Banzinni.'

'Oh him.' Thomas Dolan scratched his head. 'Come to think of it,' he said, 'I remember reading that his nickname is Pug. Of course, he was a boxer at one time so that would tally.'

'A boxer?' David said. 'I knew Kevin was fibbing when he told us he was a criminal. He made up that nonsense about him being in prison and that his henchmen were planning to free him.'

'Free him?' Thomas Dolan said in a puzzled voice. 'Well, I don't know about that. But Pug Banzinni is in prison. He's going to be flown back to America on Friday. I heard about it on the news. Now, I've work to do. I can't stand about here all day talking about criminals.'

He went into the milking parlour and Kevin turned triumphantly to his brother and Alan. 'There,' he said. 'Now wasn't I telling the truth?'

'So there is a man called Pug Banzinni,' David conceded. 'And he is a criminal. But I bet you made up the rest.'

He walked back to the summerhouse and Alan and Kevin followed him.

'Maybe he didn't make it up,' Alan suggested. 'Maybe Kevin is telling the truth. If he is then that criminal will get away if we don't tell someone that his henchmen are planning to free him.'

'Who would believe that story?' David asked. 'We don't have any proof that it's true.'

'We have to get proof then,' Alan said. 'Once we get proof we can take it to the police.'

'We call them gardai here,' David said. 'But how can we get proof?'

'We'll have to find Slim and Tiny,' Alan said. 'If they're going to be around here until Friday then they must have some place to stay. Once we find out where they're staying, we can spy on them. And we must find out all we can about Pug Banzinni.'

The three were growing excited at the prospect of adventure and wanted to start right away. But where could they begin? There were dozens of guesthouses scattered around the area and hotels in the larger towns. It would be impossible to check on all of them.

'I've an idea,' David said suddenly. 'The story will be on the evening paper. We can get information from that. We'll go into Charlestown and buy a copy. Come on. There's no time to lose.'

They ran back to the house and David told his mother they were going into Charlestown. Then he and Alan took the bicycles from the garage. Kevin sat up behind his brother on the carrier and they set off.

They reached Charlestown in fifteen minutes and went immediately to the newsagents. David bought an evening paper and they huddled together by the door to read it.

The story about Pug Banzinni, along with his picture, was on the front page. David read the report in a whisper. It said that Pug Banzinni was one of the most feared criminals in America. He had fled the country before he could be arrested and had come to Ireland. But he had been arrested by the gardai and put in prison. Now a judge had decided he should be sent back to America to stand trial. He would be flown out from Shannon Airport on Friday afternoon.

'Well, that's that,' David said in a disappointed voice. 'We've wasted our time. Pug Banzinni is flying out from Shannon Airport. That must be a hundred miles from here. We can't do anything to stop his henchmen from freeing him there. Slim and Tiny were only checking the airport in case he was flown out from here. They've probably gone away by now.'

Alan nodded. He too was disappointed. He had been looking forward to the adventure and thought he would have a great story to write up for the school magazine. But Kevin was most disappointed of all. It had been his very own story and now it had come to nothing.

They headed home with their spirits at a low ebb. When they reached the hill outside the town the two boys dismounted from their bicycles and Kevin walked beside them. All three were silent. There was nothing to talk about. Even David's attempt to start a conversation with Alan about going fishing failed miserably.

Just then they heard a car coming up behind them. It slowed down and Kevin thought it was the Americans' limousine. His heart leaped in his chest and he was too scared to turn around. Only when the car stopped beside him and he heard a familiar voice did he dare look.

To his relief it was only Mrs Kelly, whose mother used to live near the airport until she died last winter.

'Hello,' Mrs Kelly said. 'I see you're having a problem with the hill. If you like I'll take Kevin home. I'm on my way out to my mother's old cottage. I rented it today to two Americans.'

'Americans?' David repeated. 'Did you say two Americans?'

'That's right,' Mrs Kelly said.

'Is ... is one of them very big?' Kevin asked, 'and the other short and fat?' He tried to keep the excitement out of his voice but failed. 'Do they dress all in black and have a large car?'

'That's them,' Mrs Kelly said, nodding. 'They're making a film at the airport. Can you imagine that? They've taken the cottage because it has a large shed where they can keep their car.'

'Are they renting the cottage for long?' David asked.

'Until this Friday,' Mrs Kelly said. 'I'm on my way there now to see if Pa Mack has delivered a trailer of turf. They'll need it to heat the water. I'm actually glad I met you. You see I need someone to put the turf in the shed for me. I suppose you wouldn't mind doing that?'

'We wouldn't mind at all,' David said. 'In fact, we'd be delighted.'

'Oh,' Mrs Kelly said, 'I'm glad to hear that. Well, I'd best be on my way. Tell your mother I said hello.'

They nodded, barely able to stop themselves from whooping. They said goodbye to Mrs Kelly and assured her that Kevin would be fine with them. It was only when she had driven away that they could vent their feelings.

'It's them!' David exclaimed. 'They've given Mrs Kelly the same excuse about making a film as they gave Cathy. And if they're staying until Friday then the airport here must be part of their plan. Now that we know that, we can make further investigations. We'll have a great opportunity when we go there to put in the turf.'

'The airport here is somehow involved in their plan all right,' Alan said. 'But in what way? If Pug Banzinni is flying out from Shannon what can Knock have to do with it?'

'I don't know,' David said. 'But we can find out. We must get Kevin to tell us everything he overheard. Maybe we'll have an idea of what they're up to then.'

'It'll be a great adventure,' Alan said. 'I can hardly wait to begin.'

They all agreed that it was going to be terribly exciting. They might even get their names on the paper or appear on television if they prevented Pug Banzinni from escaping.

'We'll have to be careful,' David warned. 'We'll be dealing with very dangerous men.'

'That's right,' Kevin said. He was still thinking of his narrow escape that afternoon.

'We'll start our investigation tomorrow,' David said. 'We've only got four days left. Now we mustn't tell anyone what we're doing. Not until we know what they're up to. Let's shake hands on that.'

The three shook hands. Then Kevin climbed up on the carrier of David's bicycle and they shot off up the hill. If Mrs Kelly saw them now she would be amazed at where they had suddenly got the energy from.

5

# KEVIN'S NIGHTMARE

When they arrived home they went to the summerhouse, where Kevin recounted what he had heard at the airport.

'I remember they said that the runway was long enough for a jumbo jet to land,' Kevin said, his small face pursed up as he tried to recall everything. 'They also talked about a helicopter and a hearse and a decoy. Only, I don't understand what that word means.'

'It's using a bait to lure someone or something,' Alan said.

'But who would they want to lure?' David asked.

'We don't know,' Alan said. 'We'll have to make it top of our list of things to find out. But there's so much more. If the jumbo jet carrying Pug Banzinni is flying out from Shannon, why did they say that the runway here is long enough for a jumbo jet to land? And what do they want a helicopter and a hearse for? They are strange things to want.'

'Maybe the jumbo jet is the decoy,' David suggested. 'They might be planning to swop planes?'

'The decoy could be the helicopter,' Alan said. 'We just don't know.'

'I know,' Kevin said excitedly. 'They're going to free Pug Banzinni from prison and bring him to the airport by helicopter. They'll have a jumbo jet here then to fly him to America.'

'But what do they want a hearse for?' David asked.

'In case someone is killed,' Kevin said, trying to be helpful.

David and Alan exchanged looks and grinned. 'Dumbo,' David said. He playfully punched Kevin on the arm. 'What are you?'

'They'd have to bury them, wouldn't they?' Kevin said defensively.

They grew silent now, deep in thought. Outside, dusk was thickening and pressing against the windows. To the west the sun, a red ball of fire, had just slipped below the horizon. Nephin and its smaller neighbouring hills were silhouettes against the lighter sky.

'There's nothing more we can do tonight,' Alan said eventually. 'So we must decide what we are going to do tomorrow.'

'I'll ask Dad if we can put in the turf for Mrs Kelly tomorrow,' David said to Alan. 'If he agrees, then you and I will go along to the cottage in the morning.'

'What about me?' Kevin demanded.

'They know you,' David said. 'If they saw you they'd be suspicious.'

'But we'd need to know for certain if they are the same two men Kevin saw at the airport,' Alan pointed out. 'The only ones who can tell us that are Kevin or Cathy.'

David nodded. 'You're right,' he said. 'We'll take Kevin along with us. He can confirm if the two men at the cottage are the same ones he saw at the airport. But we must make sure that the Americans don't see him.'

They agreed on this. They would cycle to the cottage in the morning and Kevin could confirm the two Americans were the men he had seen at the airport. If they were, then they could begin investigations to find out what part Knock Airport had to play in the plan to free Pug Banzinni. Satisfied that this was all they could do for now, they returned to the house.

There, David sought out his father and asked if they could put in the turf for Mrs Kelly.

'You can do it in the morning,' Thomas Dolan said. 'Then, since it's Alan's first day here, you can have the afternoon off. But I want you all in the bog on Wednesday.'

'Thanks, Dad,' David said. Later that night when they were in their bedroom he told Alan and Kevin that everything was set for the morning.

Kevin found it hard to sleep that night. He tossed and turned in bed, his mind filled with the dangers he might encounter. Sleep eventually claimed him but there was to be no relief from his fears.

In his dreams Kevin again found himself back in the JCB. Outside the window the faces of Slim and Tiny loomed large and distorted. They were going to cut out his tongue. He was terrified and pleaded with them not to. But they laughed at him. They said they would take him away and lock him up in a dark outhouse where there were rats that would nibble and bite him, and cockroaches that would crawl all over him.

The door of the cab slowly opened and a hand reached inside. Kevin shrank away from it and crouched up tight in a ball. Slowly the hand crept nearer and nearer. Suddenly it shot forward and grabbed his shoulder. He jerked with fear and cried out: 'No, don't take me!'

'It's all right, Kevin. It's OK.'

The hand still gripped his shoulder and when he opened his eyes he saw a figure loom above him. He opened his mouth to scream again but just then a shaft of moonlight lit up the figure's face. To Kevin's relief he saw it was David.

'It's all right,' David reassured him. 'You're having a nightmare.'

'I thought it was them,' Kevin whispered. 'They were going to lock me up with rats and cockroaches.'

'There's nothing to worry about now,' David went on. 'They aren't going to get you. Go back to sleep. We'll have to be up early.'

'I'm OK now,' Kevin said. 'I won't have any more nightmares.'

Nothing more disturbed their sleep and the sun was shining through the bedroom window when they awoke the next morning. As they washed and dressed they could hardly hide their excitement. In the kitchen they tucked into muesli, boiled eggs and home-made bread, all washed down with tea and milk.

'I suppose you're off to put in the turf for Mrs Kelly now?' Thomas Dolan asked.

'We are, Dad,' David answered.

'And what are you doing today, Kevin?' his father asked him.

'Kevin's coming with us,' David said quickly. 'He's going to help us.'

'Can I come with you too?' Cathy asked.

'We don't mind,' Alan said, before anyone could protest.

'Very good,' Thomas Dolan said. 'Now be careful on those bicycles.'

They left shortly afterwards, promising to return for lunch. David asked Alan why he'd agreed to let Cathy come with them. Alan explained they would need a lot of help and that Cathy should be told what they knew. David agreed to this and while they cycled along, they told Cathy everything.

At first she refused to believe them. 'I met the Americans yesterday,' she said. 'They told me they were making a film. I made Kevin promise not to mention a word to anyone. And now look what he's done.'

'You shouldn't have made me promise that,' Kevin protested. 'It wasn't fair. They are criminals and they're planning to free Pug Banzinni.'

'It's true, Cathy,' Alan said. 'We'll show you the paper later. Now the important thing is that you know what's happening. It could be dangerous and we might have to make a quick getaway. So if anything goes wrong, cycle away from there as fast as you can.'

The urgency in Alan's voice convinced Cathy that he was serious and she promised to do as he said. They didn't speak again. Their thoughts now were solely occupied with the terrible dangers that might lie ahead.

Soon they saw the steel structure at Knock Airport containing the guidance equipment at the end of the runway. They passed the road leading to the airport and dipped down round a sharp bend. Now they had to climb a much steeper hill and it took all of Kevin's strength to push around the pedals of his BMX. At the top of the hill David led them to the left onto a narrow tarred road. After a few hundred yards he stopped and they gathered around him.

'There's the bank of turf we have to take out to the roadside,' he said, pointing into the bog. 'The cottage is further along on the right-hand side. It's the one with the shelter belt of spruce trees. David and myself should cycle along there on our own. We don't all want to be seen together. We'll find out if the Americans are there and if there's any sign of danger. Then we'll come back and let you know. You'll wait here until we return.'

They agreed to this and David and Alan set off again. Now that they were close to the cottage the tension increased. Their grips tightened on the handlebars and their knuckles showed white. They rounded a bend and saw the trees up ahead.

'There's the cottage now,' David whispered to Alan. 'Keep your eyes open.'

They passed the cottage, a long low building with three windows and a door at the front. Further on there was a farm gate giving access to a range of outbuildings and sheds. Outside one shed there was a heap of turf. Parked inside the gate was a black limousine. But there was no sign of anyone.

They cycled past and didn't stop until the next bend took them out of sight of the cottage.

'Well?' David asked urgently when they'd dismounted. 'Did you see anyone?'

'No.' Alan shook his head. 'But that limousine is like the one we saw yesterday parked along the road to the airport.'

'We have to be certain,' David said. 'The only ones who can tell us if it is the same limousine are Cathy and Kevin.'

'They'll have to cycle by like we did,' Alan suggested. 'That's the only way we'll find out for sure.'

'I know,' David said. 'But it could be dangerous.' He looked across the fields and the heather towards the airport. The orange windsocks along the edge of the runway were gently blowing in the warm breeze. All seemed quiet. Yet if their suspicions were correct, a great drama would be played out there on Friday. They were the only ones who possessed knowledge of it. If they didn't act then a notorious criminal might escape.

'We'll go back,' David said. 'Maybe we'll get a glimpse of them.'

They cycled slowly past the cottage but again there was no sign of the Americans.

'We'll go on back to Cathy and Kevin,' David suggested. 'Then we can decide what to do next.'

When David and Alan got back they all huddled together to discuss what they should do next. They were so engrossed that at first they didn't hear the engine noise of an approaching car. It was almost upon them when Alan heard it. He turned his head and recognised the limousine which had been parked at the cottage. He nudged David who in turn nudged Kevin. Kevin turned to face the road just as the car passed. It was travelling slowly and as it went by the man in the passenger seat glanced at them. Kevin recognised him immediately. It was Slim. He was holding what appeared to be a map in his hands. Tiny, who was driving, had a large cigar stuck in his mouth.

'It's … it's them,' Kevin said, not daring to raise his voice above a whisper. 'The driver is Tiny. The other one is Slim.'

'I recognise them too,' Cathy said. 'But could we be making a mistake? Is it possible they are making a film about Pug Banzinni? Films are made about real criminals, you know.'

'They could be,' Alan said. 'That's what we have to find out. Now I suggest that David and I go along to the cottage and start putting in the turf. While we're doing so we'll take a good look around.'

'Can Kevin and I do something to help?' Cathy asked.

'Maybe you could get us today's paper,' Alan suggested. 'There might be something in it about Pug Banzinni.'

'We could get it at the airport,' Kevin said.

'That's a good idea,' David said. 'You never know what you might learn there. Now, Alan and I will start on the turf. When we're finished we'll come straight home. Then we can discuss what we've learned so far.'

With agreement reached on how they should proceed, they split up. Alan and David headed for the cottage while Cathy and Kevin set off for the airport.

## 6

# A DOUBLE ENCOUNTER

When Cathy and Kevin reached the airport the security guard at the gate told them to leave their bicycles beside his hut and he would keep an eye on them. They thanked him and did as he said.

It was quiet at the airport. There were only a few dozen cars in the car park. Cathy and Kevin looked around for the Americans' limousine but it was nowhere to be seen. But as they entered the terminal building they saw it. It was parked in a place reserved for airport personnel. The security guard close by was clearly ignoring this breach of airport regulations.

'The Americans must be very important,' Kevin said. 'Only important people are allowed to park there.'

'They must be inside,' Cathy said. 'Let's see if we can find them.'

Kevin nodded. He wished he hadn't suggested coming to the airport. What if the Americans saw him and knew he was a spy? As they entered the terminal building he lowered his head and clenched his mouth tight shut to ensure his tongue didn't accidentally pop out. But once inside there was no sign of Slim or Tiny. Cathy bought a paper and they checked through it for any news of Pug Banzinni. On an inside page they found what they were looking for. But the piece was very brief and merely told them what they already knew.

Kevin was disappointed. He had hoped there might have been a clue in the paper as to what Slim and Tiny were planning to do. Now the hope was dashed. Despondent, he glanced up from the paper. He was struck dumb with fear. There, not ten yards away, were the two Americans. They were chatting to a third man. The two shook hands with this third man who entered an office close by. A notice on the door said 'Manager'. Meanwhile the two Americans headed for the exit. They hadn't seen Cathy or Kevin.

Kevin took a deep breath and nudged his sister. 'It's ... it's them,' he managed to gasp. 'They've just gone outside.'

'Come on,' Cathy whispered. 'But be careful.'

They walked quickly to the exit doors and slipped outside. They were just in time to see the limousine disappear up the ramp leading to the car park. They ran up the steps and as they reached the top saw the limousine go out through the exit gate. It turned right and disappeared from view.

'They were talking to a tall man with grey hair,' Kevin said. 'He was wearing glasses. He must work here because he went into an office with the word "Manager" on the door.'

'Maybe he's an accomplice?' Cathy pondered.

'What's an accomplice?' asked Kevin .

'Someone who helps with a crime,' Cathy explained. 'There's nothing we can do here now,' she added. 'So we'd best go home.'

They crossed the car park to the exit and the security man came out of his hut to meet them.

'Got your passport?' he asked Kevin. 'You can't board the shuttle to the moon without it.'

Both Kevin and Cathy laughed. 'I'm the captain of the shuttle,' Kevin said. 'I don't need a passport.'

'Oh very sorry, Captain.' The security guard saluted smartly.

Kevin roared with laughter as they retrieved their bikes and this cheered Cathy. She hated to see her brother upset and he had been disappointed by their failure to find any clues. Just then a thought struck her.

'Who is the tall grey-haired man who works here?' she asked.

'That's the airport manager,' the security guard answered.

'And who are the men in the limousine?' Kevin asked.

'Why would you want to know that?' The security guard became suspicious.

Kevin was about to reply when Cathy quickly intervened. 'We don't want to know,' she said. 'What Kevin means is that we wanted to speak to them. They're tourists and they're renting Mrs Kelly's cottage. Our brother and cousin are putting turf in the shed for them. I thought if we saw them we could tell them about it.'

'Tourists!' The security guard laughed. 'They're not tourists. They're from Hollywood. They're going to make a film here at the airport.'

'Oh I see,' Cathy said. 'Well, thank you for watching our bicycles. Come on, Kevin,' she added. 'We'd best be getting home.'

'Goodbye, Captain,' the security guard said, saluting smartly again.

'Goodbye,' Cathy and Kevin said together. They mounted their bicycles and set off home. They felt now that the journey hadn't been wasted. The airport clearly had a part to play in the plan to free Pug Banzinni. If it hadn't, then Slim and Tiny would have gone away by now. Obviously they were pretending to be making a film as part of the plan. But what could that plan be? How did they intend to free Pug Banzinni? What part did Knock Airport have to play in it? Until they had answers to those questions there was little that could be done.

As they reached the T-junction and turned for home, Cathy hoped David and Alan were having better luck. If they didn't get some information soon as to what the plan was, then there was little they could do to stop it from succeeding. Pug Banzinni would fly out from Shannon three days from now. They had only 72 hours left.

At the cottage David and Alan made a start on the turf. They worked quickly and soon there was a large pile of turf in the shed.

'It's time I looked around,' David said. 'I'd best do it before Slim and Tiny return. Keep a look out and if you see anything suspicious, give a warning whistle.'

With Alan keeping a look out, David began his investigation with the outbuildings. Apart from the turf shed which contained a ladder, there was a cow byre with bales of hay thrown in a corner and a few empty bags that had once contained potatoes. Beside the byre was a large shed with wooden doors. The hasp was secured by a padlock. Mrs Kelly had said the Americans had wanted the shed for their limousine. But they hadn't kept the car there. So what did they want it for?

What had they hidden there or were about to hide there?

David slipped through the gap in the hedge which separated the cottage from the outbuildings. He found himself in the garden, which was overgrown. Beneath the hedge, nettles and weeds flourished. The cottage was dilapidated. So why had the Americans chosen it? It had to be because it was close to the airport and was isolated and secluded.

David stealthily circled the cottage, peering through each window in turn. But he could see little through the net curtains. It wasn't until he reached the rear of the cottage that his luck changed. Here an extension with a flat roof and one chimney had been added. It had two windows, one of which didn't have curtains. David peered into this room. It was the kitchen.

A newspaper was thrown on the table. It was upside down but David could make out the word Banzinni. He was on the right track. He moved along to the other window in the extension. This window consisted of a fixed pane of glass with a small hinged opening at the top. The glass was frosted and he could not see in. He knew this must be the bathroom window.

The top part was hinged open. The aperture was tiny but a small child would be able to wriggle through. David was considering what to do next when he heard a shrill, urgent whistle. Were the Americans returning already? he wondered with a stab of fear. If they were to catch him snooping ... He remembered Kevin's nightmare and shivered. He hesitated and then ran back to Alan. But the danger signal had come much too late. As he dashed through the opening in the hedge he almost collided with the limousine.

The engine died and the doors opened. The Americans got out.

'What's goin' on here?' Slim demanded. He was frowning and his eyes were narrowed with suspicion. His bald head glistened with sweat.

'They're snoopin',' Tiny said. 'Will I give them a darn good hidin'?' His small mean eyes lit up and his suit bulged as he flexed his muscles.

'Naw.' Slim held up his hand. 'They got tongues, I reckon. Let's see what they gotta say for themselves.' David and Alan exchanged glances. Both tried not to betray their fear.

'We're putting in the turf,' David said quickly. 'Mrs

Kelly asked us to.'

'Mrs Kelly, eh?' Slim rubbed his big nose. The veins looked like piped blue icing on a novelty cake. 'You must be the two boys she told us about.' He nodded slowly. 'Best get on with it, then.'

'Aren't you gonna ask him what he was doin'?' Tiny said. He pointed an accusing finger at David.

'I was thirsty,' David said. 'I was looking for a drink.'

'We'll get you a drink,' Slim said. 'I bet it's thirsty work, eh?' He laughed and walked off through the gap in the hedge, followed by Tiny. They were arguing. Slim's voice was raised in anger.

'We've got nothin' to worry about,' he said. 'They're only doin' a job. We'll be well gone by Friday.'

If Tiny answered they didn't hear him. Clearly the Americans had gone into the cottage.

'Come on,' David said. 'We'd best get busy.'

They were both shaken by the encounter and hid their fear by working at a terrific rate. While they worked Alan told David that he hadn't signalled him in time because the limousine had come from the other direction and surprised him.

Tiny brought them two glasses of water and they thanked him. 'Never mind that,' he threatened. 'You get the job done and get outa here. I got no time for snoopers.'

He threw them a baleful look and walked away.

As they gratefully drank the water Alan asked David in a whisper if he had discovered anything.

'I'm afraid not,' David said. 'I need to get inside. If I searched the cottage I might find something.'

'Break in!' exclaimed Alan in horror. 'That's against the law.'

'There's no other way,' David said. 'The bathroom window is open and someone small could get in.'

'You can't break in,' Alan protested. 'We'd get into serious trouble. Look, we'd best get on with the job for the moment. They might be watching. Tiny is very suspicious.'

They set to work again. It was warm and the sweat stuck their T-shirts to their backs. After half an hour they decided to take a rest. They were stretched out on the grass when they heard footsteps approach. It was Tiny. He towered above them like a giant black exclamation mark. The sun threw his shadow on their faces.

'I kinda stink a bit under my arms,' Tiny said. 'I need to take a bath. Only the stove's gotta be lit to heat the water. Can one of you light it?'

David leapt to his feet. All his tiredness was gone. Here was a great opportunity to get into the cottage.

'I'll light it,' he said. 'I know all about those ranges.' He gathered up an armful of turf and, after winking at

Alan, followed Tiny into the cottage.

Slim was seated at the kitchen table. He had a map spread out before him and was marking it with a red pen. He glanced at David and hastily turned the map over so it couldn't be seen. David placed the turf on the floor and opened the door of the firebox.

'I need kindling,' he said to Tiny, who watched him with distrust. 'There might be some in the big shed.'

Tiny's little eyes seemed to shrink even more. They were like gulls' eyes, two small black buttons set in a plump face.

'You better check then,' he said. 'The key's hangin' there by the door.'

David managed to conceal his elation. Here was a chance to look in the shed. But if there was anything suspicious there, surely Tiny wouldn't let him look? Before Tiny could change his mind, David grabbed the key and ran out. He winked at Alan again and received a look of amazement in return.

David opened the padlock and pulled one door slightly ajar. It was dark in the shed and after the bright sunlight, it took a few moments for his eyes to become accustomed to the murk. But as they grew used to it he saw the shed was almost empty. There was only a heap of sticks in a corner along with a broken chair and an old washing machine.

Disappointment gripped him, though he hadn't expected to find anything. They couldn't have hidden an aeroplane or a helicopter in the shed. A hearse might have fitted but why would they want one? He was certain that Kevin was mistaken there. Casting aside his disappointment he gathered up some sticks and went back out and relocked the door.

Back in the kitchen he lit the fire. But as he closed the draught and set the damper, great puffs of smoke billowed out of the range.

'You lunkhead,' Tiny shouted. He rushed at David with his fists clenched. His small black eyes now bulged in their sockets. 'You told me that you knew how to work that stove.'

'It's not my fault,' David protested. 'It's the chimney. The birds must have built a nest in it.'

'Well, stop that smoke,' Tiny ordered. He waved his arms as the smoke billowed in his face and made him cough and splutter. Slim mumbled angrily and got up from the table. He left the kitchen, taking the map with him.

David took the cover off the firebox and poked at the fire with the poker, killing the flame. Then he replaced the cover and retreated to the door as the kitchen filled up with smoke. Tiny had already slipped outside where he glared at David.

'If I thought for one moment you did that deliberate-
ly ...,' he threatened.

Just then Slim came out and David noticed he didn't
have the map with him.

'Looks like you're not gonna be able to take a bath,'
Slim said. 'I reckon we'll go and have us a bite to eat.
'Say,' he added to David, 'do you think you could clear up
whatever's blocking that chimney?'

David nodded.

'You do what has to be done,' Slim told him.

'Lock up, Tiny, an' we'll get goin'.'

Tiny glared at David but did as he was told. Then he
followed Slim out to the limousine. A moment later
David heard the limousine roar away. As it did so, Alan
came running to see what was up.

David told Alan what had happened. 'I'd like to see the
map Slim had,' he said. 'I'm sure it's got a vital part to play
in their plan. Anyway we've got a job to do. There's a
chimney needs unblocking. Let's get the ladder.'

They carried the ladder from the turf shed and placed
it against the wall of the extension.

'Careful,' David warned. 'The guttering here is made
of plastic. We don't want to damage it.'

With the ladder safely in position David climbed up
on the roof and crossed to the chimney. But he was sur-

prised to find the chimney pot was covered with a steel grill. Whatever was causing the chimney to smoke, it wasn't a bird's nest.

'It must be the flue of the range that's blocked,' he said to Alan when he came back down. 'I'll have to clean it from inside.'

'Well, we can't do anything about that,' Alan said.

'Can't we?' asked David. 'Well, I've got an idea. Slim told me to clear up the problem and that's what I'm going to do. I'll call on Mrs Kelly and borrow a spare set of keys. Then I can get inside without being accused of breaking in. I'll check the flue and take a look around as well.'

'You ... you wouldn't dare,' Alan said in disbelief. 'What if Slim or Tiny find out?'

'They won't,' David said. 'Even if they find out, what can they do about it? You do whatever has to be done, Slim said to me. That's all I'll be doing. Now you wait here and I'll cycle down to Mrs Kelly's. Then we'll see what those two are really up to.'

# 7

## EVIDENCE DISCOVERED

Mrs Kelly was alarmed to learn of the problem at the cottage.

'I'm glad you can help me,' she told David. 'Indeed I wonder if you would take the job of caretaker? I'll give you a set of spare keys. Only I don't have the one for the front door. I've lost it. You could do all the odd jobs about the place. I'd pay you for every job you did.'

David couldn't believe his luck. Everything was turning out better than he could have expected. Not only would he have the keys but he would be earning extra pocket money as well. Now he could search the cottage easily.

On the way back from Mrs Kelly's David called home. He told his mother he and Alan wouldn't be home for lunch and she made sandwiches for them both.

David told Cathy and Kevin the developments. Cathy in turn explained what they had discovered at the airport.

'If they were just making a film,' David said, 'they wouldn't have been so suspicious of us today. They were really frightened we might discover what they were up to.'

'What do we do now?' Cathy asked.

'I'm going back to the cottage,' David said. 'I want to try and find that map.'

'It'll be dangerous,' Cathy warned. 'If you're caught they'll know you are up to something. There's no knowing what they might do then.'

At this David realised the seriousness of what he proposed to do. But he didn't hesitate. 'I'm going through with it,' he said eventually. 'It's my best chance of finding out something.'

'Let Kevin and I come with you,' Cathy pleaded. 'We can keep a look out.'

'OK,' David agreed. 'I'll search the cottage and you can keep a watch with Alan and Kevin. If you see the Americans returning you can warn me and I'll get out of there quickly.'

'But how will we signal to you?' Cathy asked. 'We'd need to keep watch from the top of the hill in order to see the road in both directions. It's too far to run back to the cottage to warn you.'

This unforeseen problem cast gloom on the proceedings. This time Kevin had the solution to the problem. 'We could use the walkie-talkies,' he said.

'That's it!' Cathy said. 'Well done, Kevin! One of us can stay at the cottage with one set while the other two keep a look out. If the Americans return we can alert the person at the house.'

'Perfect,' David said. 'I'll get the walkie-talkies. I'd better bring a torch with me, too. Hurry now, we've no time to lose.'

A few minutes later they set off. When they reached the cottage they told Alan of their idea while he and David ate the sandwiches. Alan thought it was an excellent idea. When their hunger was satisfied, they tackled the remainder of the turf and soon had it all in the shed. Now they were ready.

They decided that Alan would remain at the cottage while Cathy and Kevin kept watch on the hill.

'They know the road much better than you,' David explained. 'Now, are we ready?'

They were ready. David looked at his watch. 'I suggest we synchronise watches,' he said. 'We'll give Cathy and Kevin ten minutes to get to the look-out spot. When they get there they will signal us with a bleep on the walkie-talkie. Only then will I go into the cottage.'

Carefully they synchronised their watches. Alan instructed Cathy on how to operate her walkie-talkie. Then Cathy and Kevin set off, their faces set with determination.

At the top of the hill they climbed over the low stone wall and crept along in the heather until they reached a clump of furze. It offered a perfect hiding place. From here they could see the road in both directions for more than a mile. But in his excitement Kevin forgot about the prickly bits on the furze. He sat down on a large piece and found that 1,000 ants seemed to be stinging his behind at once.

'Ow!' He leapt to his feet with a screech of pain and began to dance about like someone demented. A piece of furze covered with flowers was stuck to the back of his shorts like a ragged yellow tail.

'Ow, ow,' he continued to screech. 'Oh, the pain. Take it off me.'

Cathy managed to calm him down. 'Sshhh,' she warned. 'We're supposed to be quiet. Now stand still while I remove the furze.'

Kevin hopped from one leg to the other as Cathy removed the offending piece of furze. All the time he kept going: 'Ow, ah, ooh.' When it was over he rubbed his bottom tenderly and this time he took care to check the spot where he intended to sit.

They settled themselves in their hideout and Cathy took the walkie-talkie from her pocket. She switched it on and pulled out the aerial to its full extent. She then pressed the red signal button. The speaker bleeped and now she waited for Alan's signal. It came almost instantly.

Back at the cottage David and Alan stared at each other. They were tense and David licked his lips.

'This is it,' he said. 'I think I'd best not delay any longer. They may return any moment.'

Alan nodded. He was to remain in the garden, hidden from the road. If Cathy gave the danger signal he would bang on the rear door of the cottage to warn David, who had made his way to the rear of the cottage. He unlocked the kitchen door and pushed it open. He hesitated a moment and took a very deep breath. Then he entered the kitchen.

He looked round the room, wondering where to start. Eventually he began with the dresser. But the search proved fruitless. He examined the cassette recorder which sat on the dresser. But it yielded no clue. Next he searched the cupboards and the fridge and gas cooker. He even opened the oven door of the range and looked inside. But it was empty. He checked the flue and saw that it was blocked with soot. He would deal with that some other time. For now he would concentrate on his search.

He listened at the closed door which led into the living-room. But he could hear no sound. Carefully he opened the door and listened again before venturing into the room. But the cottage was both empty and silent. The only sound he could hear was the beat of his own heart.

He searched the living-room but without success. Off the living-room there was a door leading to a bedroom and a door leading out to the hall. David chose this latter door.

Off the hall was the bathroom and two other bedrooms. The bathroom yielded no clue and he moved on to the bedrooms. Here there was a smell of must and damp. The beds were clearly not in use. David checked under the beds but the beam of his torch only disturbed a spider which scurried to safety. He checked the wardrobes and the dressing-table drawers but they were empty. Lastly he checked under the mattresses but found nothing.

He returned to the living-room and stood listening for a moment, all tensed up and ready to flee at the slightest sound. But silence surrounded him like a barrier. Only his heart boomed in his chest like a drumbeat.

The door to the remaining room beckoned him. But he hesitated. If this room offered no clue then all was lost. Gulping with anxiety, David opened the door to the last bedroom and stood on the threshold. The curtains were drawn and the room was gloomy. For a moment he imagined that someone, it appeared to be a giant man, crouched in the far corner. But as he choked back his kindling terror, he realised it was only a shadow.

He switched on his torch and played the beam around the room, taking care to avoid the window. He didn't want to betray his presence to a casual passer-by. The room contained two single beds, both in a state of disarray. Clearly Slim and Tiny weren't very tidy. Their luggage, which consisted of two large leather suitcases, lay on the floor. David searched both suitcases but they contained only clothes and personal belongings.

He checked the wardrobe but it was empty. The dressing-table produced nothing either, apart from some smelly socks. The beds held only the bedclothes and though he checked under the mattresses, he knew by then that he wouldn't find anything. There wasn't even a spider under the beds. He had drawn a complete blank.

He was bitterly disappointed. He had hoped to find one clue as to what Slim and Tiny were planning. But there was no clue here, not even the map. He swung his torch around the room one last time. The beam traversed the walls below the level of the window sill and passed across the fireplace, reached the door jamb and wavered. Suddenly, with a jerk, it returned to the fireplace and stopped.

David's heartbeat quickened. There were traces of soot in the fireplace. Someone had disturbed the chimney. Could it have been birds? he thought. But the birds had built their nests months ago. This soot looked fresh. It had been disturbed in the past few days.

Quickly David crossed to the fireplace and knelt down. His heart was beating wildly now and his hands trembled with excitement. He put his head into the opening and shone the torch up the dark chimney. The light was reflected back from a shiny object. There was something up there!

He felt with his hand and discovered that a metal grill was wedged in the chimney. He caught the grill in his fingers and gave a few, sharp tugs. It suddenly became dislodged and, as it did so, a metal box fell into the fireplace. The box was heavy and solid and fell with an enormous clang which was amplified by the chimney. David was certain the noise could be heard miles away. He held his breath, not daring to move as the sound reverberated in his ears.

Slowly the silence returned. It pressed in all about him. Then a noise reached his ears from the direction of the kitchen. Someone was in the house. He was certain of it. The Americans had returned without the look-outs seeing them. They were here now creeping up on him. He froze, expecting a hand to grab his shoulder.

But then he heard a humming sound in the distance and realised it was the fridge's motor. It was the noise of the motor striking against some metal part as it switched on that he had heard. The relief he felt at this urged him to action. There was no time to lose. He put down the piece of metal he held in his hand. It was cut from the expanded metal grill used by plasterers. Then he shone the torch on the box which lay in the fireplace.

It was like a large metal cash-box and he picked it up and opened it. The map he had seen Slim marking was on top. It was a detailed map of Mayo. When he lifted up the map he saw that there were brochures underneath and a great deal of money. There were bundles of Euros and American dollars.

David examined the map first. Knock Airport was underlined. The word 'hearse' was written approximately where the cottage would be on the map and was encircled. A route was marked in red which went from this circle across Barnacougue, through Kilbride to Swinford and from there to Castlebar. From there it went on to Newport and along the coast to Mulranny. At Mulranny the word 'motorboat' was written in red and underlined. Further out on the Atlantic Ocean the words 'Spanish trawler' were also written in red.

David didn't know what to make of it all. He memorised the details as best he could, aware all the time that Slim and Tiny might suddenly return. He put the map aside and checked the brochures. One was a travel brochure which gave details of flights to New York. Friday afternoon's three o'clock flight from Shannon was underlined in red ink. The other brochure was for a company which hired out helicopters. Again David memorised as much of the details as he could.

He searched beneath the bundles of money and found a small, hard-covered notebook. It was a passport. It contained the picture of a man with a beard and moustache. When David looked closely he realised that the photo, which claimed to be that of a man named Bonetti, was in fact that of Pug Banzinni wearing a disguise. Even with the disguise, David recognised him from the picture of Pug he'd seen in the newspaper. Clearly the passport was false.

Despite his trembling fingers David took care to return everything as he had found it. Then he closed the box. He couldn't really believe his luck. He now knew for certain that the Americans were Banzinni's henchmen.

Yet he was no nearer finding out what their plan was for freeing Pug. But he was determined to find out.

He glanced at his watch and realised he had been in the cottage for over 40 minutes. It was time to get out. He placed his torch on the floor, picked up the metal grill and placed the box on it. Slowly and carefully he pushed the grill up into the chimney until it disappeared from sight. Then he jammed it there as tightly as he had found it.

He picked up his torch and shone it in the fireplace and saw that the deposits of soot had become larger. He would have to clear it up before he left. He hurried to the kitchen and just then heard an urgent knock on the back door. There was no time. He had to get out now!

He took a last look around before slipping out, closing the back door behind him. Alan was waiting and beckoned him to hurry.

'They're coming,' he whispered urgently. 'Cathy's just been on the radio to say they've turned off the Galway-Sligo road. Come on. Let's get out of here.'

David followed Alan through the gap in the hedge. They grabbed their bicycles and rode out the gate and swung left. They rode like mad until they were out of sight of the cottage. Only then did they pull into a gateway.

'Well?' Alan said. 'Did you find anything?'

David nodded and Alan grinned triumphantly. Then he pressed the signal button on the walkie-talkie and spoke to Cathy.

'Mission accomplished,' he said. 'We've been successful. Returning now to base. Over.'

'Message understood.' Cathy's excitement came over the air waves loud and clear. 'Will meet you back at base. Over and out.'

Alan and David now swung back onto the road and freewheeled down hill. David was worried about the soot. He could only hope it wasn't noticed. If it was, then Slim and Tiny would know that someone had been in the cottage.

Would they guess who that someone was? He hoped not. Tomorrow he would have to return to clean the flue. If they suspected he was the person who had been in the cottage there was no knowing what they might do. They would all have to be extra careful from now on.

# 8

# A BRILLIANT IDEA

They met in the summerhouse and David recounted the details of what he had discovered at the cottage. Now that they knew for certain that Slim and Tiny were involved in the attempt to free Pug Banzinni, they became aware of the dangers they were exposing themselves to.

'We should go to the gardai,' Cathy said. 'It's much too dangerous for us to get involved any more.'

'Cathy's right,' Alan said. Kevin agreed too.

David shook his head. 'We can't go to the gardai,' he said. 'Even if they believe us, what can they do? Slim and Tiny haven't committed any crime. Even if they are questioned, they'll claim that they're making a film. The airport manager will confirm this. They'll slip quietly away somewhere else then and we'll never discover what their plans are.'

'The gardai could look up the chimney,' Kevin suggested. 'Then they'd find the false passport and the map and all the rest.'

'They'd need a search warrant first,' David said. 'And they won't get a warrant without speaking to the Americans. If the gardai call to the cottage to question them, Slim and Tiny will know the game is up. They will disappear with the box from the chimney and even if the gardai return with a warrant there won't be anything for them to find.'

They sat in silence now, mulling over what David had just said. They realised he was right. They didn't have enough information. If they were to stop the plan from succeeding, they needed much more information. But how were they to get that?

'We need to get more information,' David said, echoing their thoughts. 'We need to know what they need a helicopter for. Not to mention the hearse and the decoy. What's the significance of the route marked on the map? What part has the motorboat and the Spanish trawler got to play in it all?'

'I know,' Kevin said. 'Pug wants to go fishing when he gets out.'

The other three laughed. 'Don't be stupid, Dumbo,' David said.

'I'm not a dumbo,' Kevin protested. But he decided it might be best to stay quiet for the moment.

There was silence again. Suddenly Cathy shouted out: 'I've got it!' The others jerked to attention at her outburst and turned to stare at her. 'They're going to rescue Pug on the way to Shannon Airport,' she said, 'and put the decoy Kevin heard them talking about in his place. That way no one will know he's escaped. They'll bring the real Pug here by helicopter where he can catch a flight to England.'

'So why then is that route marked on the map?' David said. 'What do they need the motorboat and the trawler for?'

'It's to fool the gardai,' Alan said. 'They'll leave the map where the gardai can find it,' he went on. 'They'll then think that Pug is trying to escape on a Spanish trawler. While they're looking for him, he'll be making his escape by plane.'

'That's it,' Cathy nodded. 'Don't you agree, David?'

David wasn't so sure. Pug Banzinni would have a garda escort to the airport. How could he be rescued and a decoy substituted? The garda escort would have to be substituted too. But he didn't say anything to dampen the others' spirits. He needed their help if he was going to find out what the plan really was. And he was going to find out.

'I suppose it's possible,' he said. 'But what do they want the hearse for? And remember they said that the airport here was perfect because the runway could take a jumbo jet. We know jumbo jets don't fly from here to England, or to anywhere else. I think you're right when you say that Pug Banzinni is going to come here. Obviously the airport has a major part to play in the plan.'

'So we just need more information,' Alan said.

'If only we could eavesdrop on them,' Cathy suggested.

'Could one of us hide in the cottage?' Alan wondered.

David shook his head. 'It would be too dangerous,' he said. 'If we were caught, there's no knowing what Slim and Tiny might do.'

At this they grew despondent. Time was running out. They would have to go to the bog tomorrow. That left little time for further investigations.

'We have to find out what the plan is by Friday,' David said. 'After that it'll be too late. Now I have to call to the cottage tomorrow to clean out the flue of the range. I might overhear something that will help us.'

They cheered up a little at this and trooped back to the house, where supper was ready. They sat at the table, each occupied with his or her own thoughts.

'Never saw such a thoughtful lot in my life,' Thomas Dolan joked. 'Are you considering the joys of putting out the turf tomorrow?'

'Could we leave it until next week, Dad?' David asked.

'No,' Thomas Dolan said. 'We have to take advantage of the weather.'

David knew it was useless to argue with his father and when they finished supper they went off to their rooms. Alan took out his diary to record the day's events and glimpsed the voice recorder.

'I've got it!' he shouted. 'I've got it!'

As both David and Kevin stared at him in amazement, Cathy came running to the door.

'I've got it,' Alan repeated, clenching his fists in triumph. 'It's a way to eavesdrop on the Americans. And we can't be caught either.'

They crowded around as Alan took the voice recorder from the drawer and held it aloft. From the looks on their faces they clearly thought he had gone mad.

'You're not suggesting that you interview the Americans,' David said, 'and ask them what they're up to?'

'Of course not,' Alan said. 'But if we hide this voice

recorder in the cottage it will tape their conversations. Then we'll learn what they're up to.'

'We'd have to hide it while they were out,' Cathy said. 'And how would we know when they'd be back? The tape could have run out by the time they returned and we wouldn't have recorded anything.'

'Not with this one,' Alan said animatedly. 'It's voice operated.'

'Do you mean you have to tell it when to go?' Kevin said.

'In a way,' Alan said. 'Look, I'll switch it on.' He pressed a button and a red light lit up. 'Now it's recording,' he said. 'But watch what'll happen if we stop talking and remain silent. Now quiet everybody.'

They held their breath, their eyes never leaving the red light. After a few seconds the light went out. 'It's gone off,' Kevin said. But no sooner had he spoken than the light came back on. 'I did it,' he exclaimed, clearly delighted with himself.

'Sshhh.' The other three shushed him. Kevin hunched his shoulders and grinned. But he stayed silent. After a few moments the machine stopped again and the red light went out. They stood watching it as if mesmerised.

'Go!' Alan said, and the red light came on again. 'There you are. It records only when you speak. Now if we hide this in the cottage it will record Tiny and Slim's conversation.'

'I'll hide it tomorrow when I go to clean the flue,' David said.

'But how will we get it back?' Cathy asked.

'We'll worry about that tomorrow,' David said. 'The important thing now is to put it in place.'

They nodded in agreement and then Cathy said good night and went off to her own room. The boys got ready for bed. But when they were under the bedclothes, they lay awake for ages thinking of what was to come. The only certainty was that there would be a great deal of danger.

# 9

# THE ELECTRONIC EAR

Next morning David and Kevin harnessed Dobber the pony, and hitched him to his cart. This had rubber wheels and was suitable for travelling on spongy bog. They loaded their provisions and, with Cathy driving, set off. Alan and David took their bicycles while Kevin rode in the cart with Cathy.

When they reached the bog they went straight to the bank of turf, which had been footed some weeks previously. Footing entailed four sods of turf being stood upright against each other to form a pyramid. A single sod was then placed across the top. This structure was called a grogin.

Hundreds of grogins stood along the bank like soldiers

on parade. They had now to be taken out to the road-side. From there Thomas Dolan would take the turf home with the tractor and trailer.

David knew every inch of the bog and he pointed out the dangers. Two drains ran along the track leading to the bank itself. The drains were deep and heather had grown over the top of them so they were traps for the unwary. Further in was a bank which was almost cut away. The rain and frost had undermined the bank and it was dangerous to venture near the edge. The ground could collapse, toppling one into the murky water.

Once the dangers were pointed out they set to work. It was hard, back-breaking work and soon their muscles ached. After two hours the heap at the roadside had grown and David called a halt.

They were glad of any excuse to rest their aching muscles and didn't need to be asked twice. While David and Kevin unhitched Dobber and gave him water and some grain, Cathy and Alan sorted out their provisions. There were chicken and ham sandwiches and soda bread, polka dotted with currants and raisins and spread with home-made jam. There were biscuits and juicy apples and flasks of tea and a bottle of lemonade.

They tucked into the food, which tasted better than any food they had ever eaten. The work and fresh air had given them appetites which the wholesome food soon appeased. When their appetites had been sated they lay down on the heather, soaking up the sunshine. Above them a lark sang, so high in the sky that it wasn't even a speck on that cloudless tent of blue. The softest of breezes cooled them and made the heads of the bog cotton dip and bob like grey-haired men nodding to each other.

They lay resting in silence for about fifteen minutes and then David sat up. Below, the countryside was spread out like a multi-coloured bedspread. To the north he could see the Ox Mountains in Sligo and as he turned his head to the left he saw the Nephin ranges out to the west and further left again the distinctive triangular peak of Croagh Patrick. Behind him lay the towns of Kilkelly and further on Knock itself.

He looked towards the airport. It was there on Friday that a dramatic, exciting and dangerous event would take place. But how was the drama to unfold? If they were to find out, he would have to act soon. It was time to put the next part of their plan into operation.

'It's time for me to go,' he said. 'The sooner I hide the recorder in the cottage the sooner we'll have the chance to find out what's going to happen. So if we're agreed, I'll go there now.'

They were all in agreement and David set off for the

cottage on his bicycle, the recorder concealed in his pocket. When he reached the cottage he discovered the limousine was missing. He walked round to the back door and immediately noted that the bathroom window was closed. Did they suspect that someone had been in the cottage yesterday evening? Had they noticed the extra soot in the fireplace?

David hesitated, his hand in his pocket on the spare set of keys. It was then he noticed the door was ajar. Someone was home. He knocked and after a few moments Tiny came to see who it was.

'Whadya want?' he growled. 'You here snoopin' again?'

'No,' David said quickly. 'I've come to clean the flue of the range.'

'Oh, yeah,' Tiny said. 'I suppose you'd best come in. Just get the job done and then clear off.' He stared at David and continued to stand in the doorway blocking the entrance.

'You didn't sneak back here last night to do some snoopin'?' he suddenly asked.

David took a step backwards. 'No,' he said. 'Why ... why do you ask?'

'Never you mind that,' Tiny said. He glared at David before standing aside to let him enter.

Once inside David busied himself with the range and soon had the flue cleaned. While he was working he furtively looked around, seeking a suitable place to hide the recorder. It would have to go where it wouldn't be noticed and at the same time be able to record clearly any conversation.

In the end he settled for a bowl containing a display of artificial flowers which stood on the dresser beside the Americans' own radio-cassette recorder. The bowl was shallow and wouldn't block out the sound. Now all he needed was an opportunity to conceal his recorder.

When the flue was cleaned he lit the fire. This time no smoke belched out to choke him. His task was now completed but he still hadn't had an opportunity to hide the recorder. Tiny had not taken his eyes from him all the time he worked. He tried to think of some excuse to get Tiny out of the kitchen. But his mind seemed clogged like a piece of rusted machinery.

Just when he thought he had failed, he heard the toot of a car horn.

'That'll be Slim,' Tiny said. 'You wait here,' he ordered David. 'Don't go sneaking off until I tell you to.'

Tiny left the kitchen and as he did so David sprang into action. He crossed to the dresser, taking the recorder from his pocket. He pressed the record button and removed the flowers from the bowl. He placed the machine in the bowl and noted that the red light was on. Then he replaced the flowers and feverishly rearranged them, ensuring that the recorder was well hidden.

He heard the approaching voices of Slim and Tiny just then and barely had time to dash back to the range before they came into the room. Tiny was carrying a small black suitcase and Slim had his usual briefcase.

'You can clear off now,' Tiny said to David. 'And see you don't come back here no more.'

David didn't need to be told twice. He was greatly relieved to get away. As he cycled back to the bog his thoughts were on the recorder at the cottage. It was listening now like an electronic ear to each and every word the Americans would speak. Everything depended on it. If it were to fail them, then all was lost.

But if only David knew it, he need not have worried. For no sooner had he left the cottage than Slim and Tiny sat down at the kitchen table to discuss progress on the plan to free Pug Banzinni. And they were being very careful. Not once did they mention Pug's name. Instead they used the name Bonetti which David had seen on the false passport.

Slim opened his briefcase and removed a number of

documents. Carefully he read through them, checking and re-checking each point. He then removed a map and instructed Tiny on the details of that part of the plan.

'Everything quite clear now, Tiny?' Slim asked when he'd finished.

'I dunno,' Tiny said. 'Maybe if you explained it all again.'

'Are you stupid or what?' Slim demanded angrily.

'It's just that I get so easily confused,' Tiny said defensively. 'I didn't go to school much. I know how to knock heads together and cut out tongues and that but I wasn't one for readin' or writin' or thinkin'. I did read a book once though. It was all about this bear that smelled horrible.'

'Pooh Bear,' said Slim who was much better educated than Tiny.

'I think it was more like a real stink,' Tiny said. 'More like the smell from a ...'

'OK. OK.' Slim said quickly. 'That's enough. Now listen carefully. I don't want to have to go over this plan again.'

Slowly Slim went over the details of the plan until Tiny agreed that he was now familiar with all aspects of it. Hidden in the bowl of flowers the electronic ear recorded every word. Just as Slim finished speaking, the tape ran out.

'I think I got it all now,' Tiny said, scratching his head. 'Only I don't seem to get to thump nobody.'

'We don't want to thump nobody,' Slim said patiently. 'We just want to do what we have to do and get away. That's all.'

'Well can I see my gun, then?' Tiny said.

'OK,' Slim said. 'If you have to.'

'Oh goody,' Tiny said. He jumped up and hefted the black suitcase on to the table. He undid the clasp and hinged open the lid. Inside there were two padded compartments and in each lay a gun, the black metal shiny with oil.

'Can I have the big one?' Tiny asked.

'You can have the big one,' Slim said in exasperation. 'Now will you close that case and put it away.'

'Sure,' Tiny said. 'I can hardly wait until Friday. I haven't had a gun in my hand in months and months.'

Slim shook his head and gathered up the papers and the map and put them back in his briefcase. He got up and passed right by the dresser, unaware that in the bowl lay a hidden recording of all the details of the plan to free Pug Banzinni.

## 10

## FURTHER DEVELOPMENTS

Late that afternoon, while the Dolans still worked on the bog, Pug Banzinni and Scarface Moran had a final meeting in the prison.

'Well,' Pug asked, 'is everything set for Friday?'

'Everything's set,' Moran said. 'Slim and Tiny have Knock Airport all sewn up. Joey and Bandy will also be there to help them. The motorboat is in position at Mulranny and the Spanish trawler is fishing off the coast. The helicopter is on hand to fly at a moment's notice. The weather is promised fine so we won't have any reason for delay.'

'What about the captain of the jumbo jet, Mulligan, isn't it? Will he do as he's told?'

Moran grinned. 'He certainly will,' he said. 'You see Captain Mulligan has a daughter called Marian who wants to be a movie star. So we've offered her a part in this movie we're not making.' He laughed and winked at Pug and looked round to make sure that the warder wasn't near. Then he leaned close to Pug and in a whisper outlined that part of the plan. 'There you are,' he concluded. 'We don't have to worry about that any more. Hal and me will be on the aircraft and we'll take care of everything.'

'I still worry,' Pug said. 'If anything goes wrong I'll spend the rest of my life in prison. Now is everything set up with the decoy?'

'It's all in hand,' Moran said. 'I've seen him and he looks perfect in the disguise. He thinks he's taking part in a movie too. He arrives at the cottage in Mayo tomorrow evening. The hearse will be brought to the cottage late tonight. We don't want anyone to see it and become suspicious. Speedy will drive it on Friday. After all, he's the best getaway driver we ever had. So you see, it's all working out like clockwork.'

'I certainly hope so,' Pug Banzinni said. 'Because if it doesn't then it's concrete socks for the lot of you.'

At this threat Moran cringed. He had a large bunion on his foot and didn't at all relish the idea of having to chip off a concrete sock. But he'd been Pug Banzinni's right-hand man for years and knew that Pug showed no mercy to anyone who let him down.

It was with apprehension that Moran said goodbye to Pug and left the prison. He was always glad when he got outside the great iron gates. He had spent many years in prison himself and hated to be locked up. He had sworn that he would never find himself locked up in prison again.

As Scarface Moran left the prison, Marian Mulligan dialled a number and listened to the telephone ring at the other end of the line. She held the receiver tightly in her hand and hoped her father, Captain Mulligan, was at home. She wanted so much to tell him the good news.

Marian was a tall girl, just seventeen years old. She had blonde hair and blue-green eyes which reminded anyone who saw them of the sea. They mostly flashed with laughter, but sometimes they looked sad. This was when Marian thought of her mother, who had died when she was a baby. She had never known her mother, except in photographs. Her favourite was the one her father kept on the sideboard at home. In this her mother's smiling face, so like her own, stared shyly at the camera. Beside it stood the photograph of her parents' wedding day. Her father stood tall and erect in his pilot's uniform.

Her mother was radiant in a white wedding dress.

Now her mother was dead and her father was greying at the temples. Sometimes, despite the distinguished marks of age, he seemed to Marian like a lost little boy. She knew he still missed her mother just as much as she missed her. It was, she often told herself, why she loved him so much. And why she was now ringing him from Dublin to tell him the good news.

She heard the click of the receiver being lifted and then her father's voice came clearly down the line from Limerick. She chatted with him for a few minutes about university. Only then did she tell him that she wouldn't be coming to see him at the weekend.

'Please don't be disappointed,' she said. 'But I've got this wonderful opportunity to appear in a movie.'

'Oh, I see,' her father said, hiding his disappointment.

'This American producer, a Mr Moran, is making a movie,' she went on excitedly, 'and he wants to give me a part in it. It's about kidnappers. I'm playing the part of a girl who's kidnapped and held for ransom. Isn't it just wonderful, Dad?'

'It sounds great,' her father said. He was delighted for his daughter. He had always known she missed her mother very much and he had tried to be both a mother and a father to her. He had taken a great interest in what she wanted to do. When she told him she wanted to be an actress, he hadn't tried to talk her out of it. Instead he'd asked her first to study for a career and this she was now doing at university in Dublin. In her spare time she worked with an amateur theatre company and had already appeared on television, much to his delight and pride. Now it appeared she was getting a big break and would be in a film. He felt he had a right to be very proud.

'I can hardly wait until Thursday when we begin rehearsals,' Marian said. 'Mr Moran said that we might be filming over the weekend so that's why I can't come down.'

'I understand,' Captain Mulligan said. 'I'm flying to New York, but when I get back I'll come and see you. So goodbye until then.'

'Goodbye, Dad,' Marian said. 'By the way,' she added, 'Pug Banzinni is going to be a passenger of yours. I read on the paper today that there might be an attempt made to free him. So make sure you take care of yourself.'

'Indeed I will,' Captain Mulligan said. 'Anyway, I won't have anything to do with him. Once he's on my aircraft, there's no way he can be freed. So there's nothing to worry about.'

'I suppose not,' Marian said. 'But you take care.' They said goodbye again, hung up and promptly forgot all about Pug Banzinni.

The afternoon Marian spoke to her father, Tiny decided to take a bath. He had sniffed under both arms and realised he now smelled as bad as the bear in that book.

'Pooh, indeed,' Tiny muttered to himself, crinkling his nose at the awful smell. 'More like the smell you get after eating a lot of beans.'

'I'm going to take a bath,' he said to Slim. 'I reckon the water should be hot.' He got his toilet bag and towels and locked himself in the bathroom. He stared at his reflection in the mirror and decided not to shave. The dark stubble gave him a mean look which he liked very much.

Humming a tune, he ran the bath and added half a bottle of pink bubble bath to the water. He then climbed in and lay down, grunting like a great sea-lion. He took his sponge and soap and washed himself. He washed the back of his neck and behind his ears and under his arms. Then he washed between his toes and tried to bite off his toenails. But after slipping down the bath and banging his head on the taps, he left his toes alone and began to play with the bubbles.

He gathered them in handfuls and blew them in the air. Then he raised them up on the tip of his big toe and tried to blow them off. But they were too far away and he didn't have sufficient wind. He soon tired of this game and decided to sing a song. But, as he didn't have a single note of music in his head, the sound he made resembled a donkey braying.

When the water became cold Tiny climbed out. He wrapped a towel about himself and dried himself vigorously. Then he got his talcum powder and dusted himself all over. Lastly he got a bottle of cologne, splashed it liberally under his arms and rubbed some behind his ears. Satisfied with that, he placed the bottle on the window sill.

He looked at himself in the mirror but the steam had condensed on the cold surface and he couldn't see properly. He wiped the glass and examined his face. He turned this way and that way, trying out a dozen mean poses. Eventually he settled on one where his eyes were narrowed and his mouth was twisted to one side. He thought it was the meanest look he had ever achieved and decided it was the one he would try at the airport when the plan to rescue Pug Banzinni was put into action.

The bathroom was filled up with steam so Tiny opened the window to let the steam out. He then got dressed and returned to the kitchen.

'There you are,' Slim said. 'If you're ready we'll go and sort out the delivery of the hearse. Ya know, I might take a bath myself when we return. Could you put some more fuel in the stove? Kinda make sure the water stays hot, eh.'

'Sure,' Tiny said and filled up the firebox. The fire had

nearly gone out and the fresh turf began to smoulder. Thick black smoke belched from the chimney.

'Let's go, then,' Slim said.

'Just a minute,' Tiny said. 'I gotta close the bathroom window.'

'Don't worry about it,' Slim said. 'Who's gonna burgle this place?'

'You've not forgotten the soot in the fireplace?' Tiny said.

'You still think someone was in here?' Slim didn't sound as if he believed it. 'We've checked and there's nothin' missing.'

'I dunno,' Tiny said. 'I've just got this feelin'. I asked that boy this mornin' if he was snoopin' around here and he looked real scared.'

'So whadya suggest?' Slim said. He was going to say that anyone would be scared of Tiny but didn't.

'Maybe I should stay behind,' Tiny said. 'You don't need me with you.'

Slim considered the matter. 'You're right,' he said. 'We can't take chances. If anything goes wrong Pug will have us all in concrete socks. OK, we'll take precautions. You stay here, then.'

'OK,' Tiny agreed. 'I think that's the best. You know, I think I'll have a lie down. The bath has made me sleepy.

I'll put the bolt on the door while you're out. If I'm asleep when you get back just knock on the window and I'll let you in.'

Slim nodded and left. Outside he smiled to himself. Old Tiny was a bit of a fusspot. But perhaps he was right. Anyway, it would be the sorry person who broke into the cottage while Tiny was on guard. They wouldn't be too anxious to break in again in a hurry.

As Slim drove away Tiny slid across the bolt on the kitchen door and went off to the bedroom. He lay down on his bed with his clothes and shoes on and soon was snoring his head off. With all his talk about security, he had forgotten to close the bathroom window.

# 11

## CAPTURE!

When they got home from the bog, the Dolans and Alan went back to the cottage in the hope of retrieving the recorder. The limousine wasn't there and after carefully checking around, they concluded that both Americans were out.

Cathy and Kevin again did look-out duty while Alan hid in the garden. Once they were all in position David crept to the rear door. He fitted the key in the lock, turned it and pushed the door inwards. But it wouldn't budge an inch. It was obviously bolted on the inside.

He felt bitterly disappointed as he crept away and told Alan what was wrong.

'They must have gone out the front door,' David said,

'and bolted the rear door. I bet they saw the soot and became suspicious. Now I don't have a key for the front door so I can't get in. We'll have to forget the whole thing.'

'My recorder is in there,' Alan said. 'I want it back. Anyway we just can't go away and forget everything. I bet the plan is there on the tape. Don't you want to know what it is?'

David nodded. 'You're right,' he agreed. 'But how are we going to get into the cottage?'

'I don't know,' Alan admitted. 'Let's go and take a look.'

They crept to the door and now David noticed the bathroom window was open again. Alan, too, noticed it.

'I know what we'll do,' he said. 'The window is large enough for a small person to wriggle through. I'd say Kevin would make it. What do you think?'

David bit his lip. He stared up into the sky as if he might find an answer there. 'I don't know,' he said. 'Wouldn't we be breaking the law?'

'Not really,' Alan said. 'After all, you have Mrs Kelly's permission to enter the cottage. Only you can't get in because the door is bolted. And you're not going to steal anything.'

'It could be risky,' David said.

'We'll have to make up our minds quickly,' Alan urged. 'We haven't got all evening, you know.'

David nodded. It was all right for Alan. Kevin wasn't his brother. But Alan was right. They had little time and if they didn't find out now what the Americans were up to, it might be too late.

'OK,' he said. 'We'll do as you suggest.'

'There's no time to lose,' Alan said. 'I'll call Cathy on the radio and tell her what's happened. She can send Kevin down here right away.'

David nodded reluctantly and, with his face creased with worry, listened to Alan give instructions over the radio. David sensed something was going to go terribly wrong. But he didn't voice his worries aloud and they waited in silence until they heard the patter of running footsteps. It was Kevin. Quickly Alan asked him if he was willing to try and get into the cottage through the bathroom window.

'Sure,' Kevin said. He was thrilled to be asked to carry out such an important mission.

'It could be dangerous,' David warned.

But Kevin wasn't thinking of danger. He had even forgotten that Tiny had threatened to cut out his tongue. Now he just wanted adventure.

'I'm not frightened,' he said. 'They don't scare me.'

'There you are,' Alan said to David. 'He doesn't mind. So let's get to work. We've no time to lose. Now there's the window, Kevin. Do you think you could get through that small opening?'

'It is very small,' Kevin agreed. 'But I'll try.'

'We'll hold your legs while you go in head first,' Alan said. 'Once you're through the opening we'll lower you onto the floor. When you've got the recorder, we'll help you back out again. OK?'

'It's going to be dead easy,' Kevin said.

'OK then,' Alan said. 'Up on the window sill, Kevin.'

Kevin climbed up on the window sill. He then reached up and grasped the bottom edge of the opening. David and Alan took a leg each and pushed upwards. Kevin put his head into the opening. He levered himself with his hands and inched his body through. It was very tight and the metal window stay was in his way. Kevin unhooked it. But the window fell down and struck him on the head. 'Ouch,' he said. 'That hurt.'

Alan and David suppressed a nervous giggle. Alan now used one hand to hold up the window. With the stay out of his way, there was nothing to obstruct Kevin. He wriggled and wiggled until most of his body was inside. He put his hands down in front of him and reached out for the wash hand basin. But he was a few inches short.

He tried to stretch a little more and felt his fingertips touch the sill. It was wet from condensation. His blood was pounding in his head and he felt dizzy. He closed his eyes and tried to stretch another inch. David and Alan felt the tug of his body and pushed his legs a little more. Kevin's fingers were now resting on the sill and he relaxed a moment.

Taking a deep breath he tried to take most of his weight on his hands. But they slipped off the wet sill and Kevin gasped with fright as he hung in mid air. He would have fallen on to the floor if his legs hadn't been held tightly. But his luck didn't hold. As he frantically scrabbled about with his hands he struck Tiny's bottle of cologne. It wobbled precariously on the very edge of the sill. Kevin made a despairing grab for it. But he only succeeded in striking the bottle, which now toppled over onto the floor. The crash of breaking glass seemed deafeningly loud. The smell of the cologne filled the bathroom and made Kevin gasp.

'Are you OK, Kevin?' David asked in a frightened whisper.

'I can't get down,' Kevin called back. 'If I go any further I'm going to fall. I ...' Kevin stopped speaking suddenly and listened. Had he heard a noise in the house? He held his breath and then he heard it again.

Somewhere a door opened. There was someone here. He heard footsteps. They were coming to get him.

'There's someone coming,' he cried. 'Help me! Please get me out of here.'

'Don't panic,' David said. 'We'll get you out.'

'Please hurry,' Kevin said. 'Oh, please help me!'

'Can I be of any assistance?'

The voice struck terror into the three of them. Outside the window David and Alan were frozen stiff like statues. Inside Kevin watched a pair of black shoes cross the bathroom floor, kicking the broken glass out of the way. A large hand grabbed his T-shirt behind his neck and an equally large hand grabbed the seat of his shorts. He was wrenched from the grip of David and Alan and a moment later he found himself standing on his own two feet looking up into Tiny's face.

'Well, well,' Tiny drawled. 'What have we got here? Don't you think you should have knocked before you came in?'

'Yes, sir,' Kevin said. 'I mean, no, sir.'

'A little burglar, eh? Don't you know what we do with burglars in the States? Eh boy, answer me.'

'I ... I don't know,' Kevin stammered. 'Do you let them go?' he added hopefully. He turned to the window but he couldn't see the dark outlines that would have told him Alan and David were there. They must have run away and left him. He was all alone. There was no one to save him now.

'Let them go,' Tiny growled. 'We certainly don't let them go. We chop them into little bits and make mincemeat out of them. Do you think you'd like that?'

'Oh, no, sir,' Kevin said. 'I ... I wouldn't like it.'

'And do you know what we do with the mincemeat?' Tiny demanded.

'Make a shepherd's pie,' Kevin said, trying to be helpful. His mother always made shepherd's pie with mincemeat.

'We feed it to dogs,' Tiny said. 'We have huge savage dogs with razor-sharp fangs. They snarl and drool from the mouth. They love mincemeat made from boys. Afterwards I like to listen to them crunching up the bones. Now if you don't want that to happen to you, you'd best tell me what you're doin' here!'

Kevin was never more frightened in his life. Being made into mincemeat was one thing. But he didn't at all like the idea of having his bones crunched up. He wished he'd stayed at home. Or else stayed with Cathy on look out. Why had he ever agreed to come in through the window? Why had he been so brave? From now on he'd be a coward. Cowards didn't get made into mincemeat or have their bones crunched up. They got to go on living.

'I'm waitin', boy,' Tiny now roared, losing his patience. Kevin jumped in the air. He looked around again, seeking a means of escape. But there was none. He was hopelessly trapped.

'I ... I came for the voice recorder,' he eventually mumbled.

'I was right,' Tiny gloated. 'You're a thief. Well I'm gonna deal with you.' He caught Kevin by the ear and dragged him into the kitchen.

'There's the recorder,' Tiny said, pointing to the radio-cassette recorder standing on the dresser beside the bowl of flowers. With each word he gave Kevin's ear a sharp tug. 'Take a good look because it's the last time you'll see it. Now I'm gonna lock you up until Slim comes back. He enjoys seeing boys made into mincemeat.'

Still holding Kevin by the ear, Tiny dragged him into one of the spare bedrooms and shut him up in the wardrobe. It was dark in the cramped space and Kevin was terrified.

'Let me out,' he screamed. 'Please let me out. I won't tell anyone. I promise.' He banged and kicked at the door. But he only heard Tiny laugh and the door of the room bang shut.

Now there was silence, except for the pounding of his heart. It seemed to beat as loudly as a drum. Then he heard gasping for breath and thought there was someone else in the wardrobe with him. Dumb with terror, he reached out with his hand to touch whoever it was. But there was no one there. The breathing he was listening to was his own.

He crouched down in one corner of the wardrobe and clenched his eyes shut, listening for any noise that would signal the return of Tiny. He didn't want to be cut up into little pieces and made into mincemeat. Nor have his bones crunched up by savage dogs. Only, if he wasn't rescued soon then that would be his fate. But he was certain of one thing. If he did get out of here alive he would never again eat shepherd's pie.

# 12

# A DARING RESCUE

When David and Alan got over their terrible fright, their first instinct was to run. They stared at each other like terrified animals facing a predator. They jumped away from the window as Kevin's feet disappeared and the window opening fell down with a loud bang.

Alan caught David's arm before he could run away.

'Stop!' he commanded in a whisper. 'There's only Tiny here. He can't catch us while he's inside. Let's wait and see what he intends to do with Kevin. OK?'

David nodded and they both crouched down beneath the window sill. Out of sight of anyone in the bathroom, they heard Tiny's angry voice and Kevin's fearful answers to his questions.

'Maybe we should get the gardai,' David suggested. 'Kevin could be in terrible danger.'

'Nothing will happen to him until Slim returns,' Alan said. 'He's the boss. Tiny won't do anything without his say so. Sshhh now. Let's listen to what they're saying.'

They heard Tiny's threat to chop Kevin up into little pieces and make mincemeat of him. Alan giggled when Kevin mentioned shepherd's pie but an angry glare from David soon put a stop to that. Then, when Kevin mentioned the recorder, their hearts leapt into their throats and fell back down again like lumps of lead. If Tiny found the recorder, he would know what they were up to. There was no knowing then what he might do.

As Tiny dragged Kevin from the bathroom, David and Alan scampered to the kitchen window. They crouched again below the sill and slowly raised their heads until they could peer into the room. They were just in time to see Tiny point to the radio-cassette recorder. At this they both breathed great sighs of relief.

But the relief was short lived, as Tiny dragged Kevin away. They heard Kevin screaming and both were terrified that Tiny might be carrying out his threat right away. So it was with great relief again that they saw Tiny come back into the kitchen.

'Come on,' Alan said. 'Kevin is safe for now. We must

make sure we don't get caught. Tiny may come out to look for us. Come on. We have to decide what we're going to do.'

They ran across the garden and through the gap in the hedge. Alan led the way to the turf shed where they leaned against the wall to get their breath back. They stood there panting for a minute, their hearts beating wildly. Slowly their heartbeats returned to normal and their breathing became more even.

'I suppose we'd best let Cathy know what's happened,' Alan said. 'She might as well come back here. There's no point keeping a look out any more.'

He spoke with Cathy on the walkie-talkie and told her what had happened. He then suggested she should return immediately. He assured her that Kevin was safe for the moment.

Meanwhile, David peered out of the shed to make sure that Tiny wasn't following them. But he knew there was no need for Tiny to do so. While he had Kevin a prisoner they were in his power.

David looked up at the sky. Already it was growing dark. They would have to act soon if they were to rescue Kevin. Slim might return at any moment and with the two thugs to deal with, they wouldn't stand a chance. If only they could lure Tiny out of the cottage, one of them might be able to sneak in and free Kevin. But how could they lure Tiny out?

David stared at the cottage and noticed the smoke from the chimney belching into the sky. Suddenly he had an idea. He grabbed Alan's arm and pointed to the smoke.

'Look,' he said. 'There's turf smouldering in the range. We can use it to help us rescue Kevin. I'll tell you what we'll do when Cathy gets here.'

When Cathy arrived they assured her again that Kevin was quite safe.

'David has a plan to rescue him,' Alan said. 'He's going to tell us all about it.'

They huddled together while David outlined his plan. They listened attentively to what he had to say and nodded to show that they understood his instructions. 'OK,' David whispered. 'Let's go.'

The dusk was thickening as David slipped out to check there was no danger. There was no sign of Tiny. David gave the all-clear signal and the other two now emerged. Cathy went off to the byre to fill one of the old potato sacks with hay. Meanwhile, David and Alan carried the ladder from the shed across to the extension. Taking care not to make any noise, they put the ladder against the wall of the bathroom where it couldn't be seen from the kitchen.

Alan ran back to the byre where Cathy had just filled a sack with hay. He grabbed the sack and ran back to the foot of the ladder with it. Meanwhile Cathy ran to the gate to keep a look out for Slim.

David grabbed the sack from Alan and quickly scrambled up the ladder on to the flat roof. He tiptoed across to the chimney, which was as tall as himself. Smoke still belched into the sky. He removed the steel grill, which prevented the birds from building nests, and hoisted up the sack of hay. Working feverishly, he stuffed the sack into the chimney pot until it was wedged tight. Then he tiptoed back across the roof and scuttled down the ladder, sliding down the last few feet.

He and Alan grabbed the ladder and lowered it to the ground. They picked it up, one at each end, and galloped with it to the turf shed. They put it back where they found it and then slipped out of the shed and hid in the byre. From here they apprehensively watched the back door of the cottage.

Back in the cottage Tiny paced the kitchen. His thick brow was creased with worry. He had recognised Kevin as the boy they had caught eavesdropping on their conversation at the airport. Did he know that they were planning to free Pug Banzinni? Did his break-in attempt have anything to do with that? Tiny's little brain couldn't cope with all the thoughts and worries as they whirled around beneath his thick skull like a funfair ride. He hoped Slim would soon return. Maybe then he could begin the punishment. He thought he might begin by cutting off one of the boy's ears. That would stop him eavesdropping.

The thought cheered Tiny up. He couldn't wait to begin. In order that there should be no delay when Slim returned, Tiny went into the bedroom and got his cutthroat razor from his shaving kit. The razor was so sharp that it could split a hair in two. But Tiny still took out the leather strap and began to hone the edge.

Suddenly Tiny stopped and sniffed the air. There was a peculiar smell. He raised each arm in turn and smelled his armpits. But there was only the scent of his cologne there. He dropped the razor and walked to the door of the living room. Now something tickled his nose and throat. There seemed to be fog in the room. It was pouring in from the kitchen.

He ran through into the kitchen which was filling up with the fog. Only it wasn't fog. It was thick black smoke and it was belching from the range. Tiny began to cough. He didn't know what to do and he panicked. He rushed to the range and opened the firebox door. A great whoosh of smoke and ashes belched out into his face. It stung his eyes and he clenched them shut. But he had to breathe and when he took a great big breath, the smoke almost choked him.

His eyes were streaming tears and when he opened them he could hardly see. He knew he had to get fresh air. He stumbled forwards but bumped his nose on the edge of the living-room door. He screeched in pain and put his hand to his injured nose. His fingers came away wet and when he held them close to his eyes he saw blood.

Tiny actually loved the sight of blood. Provided, of course, that it wasn't his own. Now the thought that he was bleeding filled him with terror. Once, when he had been ill, he had had to go to the hospital where a doctor had taken a sample of blood. At the sight of the needle and the blood Tiny had collapsed and had to be given the kiss of life. As Tiny's breath always smelled terrible, the poor nurse had never been able to kiss anyone again.

Now Tiny thought he would faint as he inched his way to the back door. He felt for the bolt and slid it across. Then he fumbled at the knob. He managed to open the door and stumble out into the air, coughing and gasping for breath. He stood for a moment to get his breath back and thought about what he should do.

He looked up at the chimney and saw there was no smoke belching out of the pot. He also saw the end of the sack sticking out.

'Must be a bird's nest,' he mumbled to himself. 'I'll have to climb up there and remove it. If I don't we won't be able to remain in the cottage tonight. Slim will go to a comfortable hotel and I'll have to sleep in the shed.' At this, Tiny trembled. He had a horrible feeling there might be rats there.

Bleeding and coughing and spluttering, Tiny stumbled to the turf shed. He took the ladder and carried it back to the cottage where he placed it up against the wall. Puffing and coughing, he climbed up on the roof and walked across to the chimney. At the sight of the sack and the metal grill which lay on the roof, a puzzled look crossed his face. He didn't know a lot about birds' nests but this appeared to be a most peculiar one. Still frowning, he caught the corner of the sack and began to pull it out of the pot.

David and Alan watched Tiny from their vantage point in the byre.

'Now!' David said urgently. 'Let's go!'

They ran across the garden, taking care not to make any noise. Tiny was busy pulling the sack out of the chimney pot and didn't hear them or see them. Making hardly a sound, they took the ladder down and laid it on the grass. Tiny was now trapped on the roof.

'Get Kevin,' David hissed at Alan. 'I'll get the recorder.'

Alan nodded and dashed into the kitchen, with David on his heels. Alan only had time to notice that the smoke was clearing now that the door was open before he ran into the hall, calling Kevin's name.

Kevin heard Alan's voice and shouted and banged on the door of the wardrobe. In a moment Alan was in the room and had the wardrobe door open.

'You're safe now,' he assured Kevin. 'But we've no time to lose. Come on.' He grabbed Kevin's arm and led him outside. David was waiting for them by the door like a deer set to flee.

Just then, a bellow of anger came from above them and they glanced up. Tiny was silhouetted on the roof against the darkening sky. He held the sack in his hands. Both his hands and his face were black from the soot.

'Put that ladder back,' he roared. 'Or I'll have you chopped into little bits when I get down.'

But the boys didn't hang about. With Tiny's bellows of anger ringing in their ears, they ran across the garden. They bumped into a frightened Cathy, who had heard Tiny's shouts and thought someone was being murdered. When she saw Kevin, relief poured into her and though she had 1,000 questions to ask, she remained silent. Not daring to delay, they retrieved their bicycles and cycled off at a cracking pace. The bicycles had dynamos fitted and they didn't have to worry about being seen in the dark. They did not once speak of their ordeal but it was uppermost in all of their minds.

Back at the cottage Tiny was stranded on the roof. He was angry and hungry. If he didn't want to remain up here for hours then he would have to climb down the drainpipe. It was the only way to get off the roof.

He lay flat on his belly on the roof and slowly slid his legs over the edge. He inched his way backwards until his legs and most of his body were hanging down. Then he reached back with his hands to grab the guttering.

It was only then Tiny realised that the guttering and drain pipe were made of plastic and wouldn't support his weight. He panicked yet again as he felt his body begin to slide off the roof. Desperately he tried to hang on but the guttering began to give way. Slowly, the plastic brackets securing it sheered off and Tiny felt himself falling. He landed on his back with a thud that knocked all the wind out of him. His head whipped backwards and struck the ladder. The last thing Tiny remembered was seeing stars in front of his eyes before he began to fall into a great bottomless pit.

## 13

## A DECISION IS MADE

They gathered in David and Kevin's room to play the tape.

Their nerves were still stretched out like pieces of elastic that might snap at the slightest provocation. Kevin felt certain the gardai would be along at any moment to arrest him. He would be sent to prison and might end up in the same cell with Pug Banzinni. The thought made him shudder.

Even David's assurances that the gardai would not come didn't do much to ease Kevin's fears.

'Slim and Tiny won't go to the gardai,' David said. 'They won't want to draw attention to themselves. Anyway, they'll assume that our motive for attempting to break in was to steal the radio cassette. They can't know that we've taped their conversation.'

'David's right,' Alan said. 'We've nothing to worry about.'

'Let's listen to the tape,' Cathy said. She was impatient to hear what was on it.

'OK,' Alan said. 'We'll do that now.' He rewound the tape and then pressed the button marked Play. At first there was a buzzing and rattling noise. Then they heard David speaking to Slim and Tiny just before he left the cottage. There was silence for a moment and then, to their relief, they heard Slim suggest he and Tiny discuss the plan to free Pug.

For 30 minutes they listened attentively to the voices of the Americans. But as each minute passed, their faces became more downcast. They didn't even laugh when Slim mentioned Pooh Bear. The two Americans had been very clever. Not once had they even hinted at the name of Pug Banzinni.

The tape reached the end and Alan switched off the recorder. There was a deathly silence while they stared at each other. The earlier tension and fear they had felt now gave way to disappointment. Here on the tape they had all the details of the plan to free Pug Banzinni. But who would believe them?

'We can't go to the gardai with that tape,' David said, breaking the silence. 'After listening to it, they would think that Slim and Tiny were discussing the plot of a film. Even if we told them what we knew they would think we were making it up.'

'I agree with David,' Alan said. 'Slim and Tiny have been very clever. We know what they're up to but we can't prove it.'

'Does that mean they will get away?' Kevin asked. His disappointment was already making him forget his ordeal of being locked in the wardrobe.

No one spoke. Three pairs of eyes stared at the floor. None of them wished to see the disappointment on Kevin's face.

'It's time for bed,' Cathy said eventually. 'We have to be up early to go to the bog.'

'You're right,' David said. He sounded resigned to failure. He yawned and rubbed his eyes with his knuckles.

Kevin couldn't believe they were going to let him down. They had risked so much and now they were going to throw it all away. He had been captured and locked up in a dark musty wardrobe. He had been threatened with having his tongue cut out. He had almost been made into mincemeat and fed to savage dogs. He'd never again be able to eat shepherd's pie and he really liked it. He'd been through all that and now they were going to let him down? Well, he'd show them!

Kevin leapt to his feet and stamped on the floor. The other three were startled and stared at him in amazement.

'Kevin!' Cathy exclaimed. 'What's come over you?'

'We have to do something,' Kevin said. 'We just can't let a dangerous criminal like Pug Banzinni escape. If the gardai won't believe us then we'll have to stop him ourselves.'

'But what can we do, Kevin?' Cathy asked.

'I don't know,' Kevin said. 'But we must do something.'

They stared at him, at the small figure with the weathered face and the blonde hair. They knew what he had been through. Just to think about it made them shiver. Yet he was the one who was still willing to risk being captured again. They now looked at each other and realised Kevin was right. They had to do something.

'We've got until Friday,' David said. 'And there can't be any harm in discussing what we could do. Does anyone have any ideas?'

Kevin clenched his fists with delight and came back to sit on the bed. For half an hour they discussed the Americans' plan in great detail.

'Now,' David said, when they had finished, 'have any of you any suggestions?'

'We can't stop whatever is going to happen at

Shannon,' Alan said. 'So we can forget about that. And we won't be able to do anything at the airport here. There will be too many of Banzinni's henchmen around and they'll be on the alert.'

'That only leaves the hearse,' David said. 'It's the key to the whole thing and the cleverest part of their plan. If we could prevent the hearse from getting away it would give the gardai time to recapture Pug Banzinni.'

'We could puncture it,' Kevin suggested. 'We know it'll be in the shed at the cottage from tonight.'

'They would see the flat tyre straightaway,' David said. 'They would just have to change it. It wouldn't delay them at all.'

'I know what we could do,' Alan said. 'We could let the water out of the radiator. They wouldn't know we'd done it. Once they start to drive the hearse the engine will soon overheat. They would then have to get water and wait for the engine to cool down. That would delay them for quite a while.'

Both Cathy and Kevin nodded their heads at this suggestion. David too eventually nodded his head.

'It's a great idea,' he said. 'It would give the gardai time to act. By then they would have been informed by the authorities at the airport of what had happened and that Pug had escaped.'

'But the gardai won't know anything about the hearse,' Alan said. 'No one knows about that but us. The gardai will go chasing the decoy and Pug will still escape.'

This pronouncement brought gloom. They seemed to be right back where they started. But then Cathy had an idea.

'One of us could go to the Garda station on Friday afternoon,' she said. 'We could tell the gardai about the hearse. They'd believe us then, wouldn't they?'

The others nodded and the gloom lifted. 'It's a very good suggestion,' Alan said. 'Once the gardai know about the hearse, they will be able to act. We'll do our part by letting the water out of the radiator. Then it will be a simple matter for the gardai to recapture Pug.'

'What if something goes wrong?' David asked. 'There will be a lot of Pug's men about. They'll be wary and dangerous. There's no knowing what they might do if they thought their plan was being thwarted.'

'But what could go wrong?' Alan said. 'We don't have anything to worry about. The gardai will be taking care of the dangerous part.'

Alan nodded. But his feeling of apprehension didn't go away. It lay in his stomach like a great mass of knotted rope. Something could always go wrong. So they would have to be vigilant and prepared for any eventuality.

'Now that we've decided on what should be done,' Alan said, 'we must draw up a plan of action. Our first priority will be to disable the hearse by letting out the water. Now, we know that it will arrive at the cottage tonight and will be kept under lock and key in the large shed.'

'I've got a key to the lock,' David said. 'So we won't have a problem getting inside.'

'So when do we let out the water?' Alan asked.

'We'll have to do that early on Friday morning,' David said. 'It'll have to be done before Slim and Tiny, and the other thugs who'll be at the cottage by then, get up. We dare not do it before Friday morning in case they check the hearse and find out what we've done. Now, as it's your idea, I suggest you should be the one to let out the water.'

'I'm willing to do that,' Alan agreed.

'So who will go to the Garda station?' Cathy asked.

'Kevin is too young to go,' David said. 'So it will have to be one of us three. Now who'll volunteer.'

'I will,' Cathy said, 'if you agree.' They all did so.

'That's settled then,' David said. 'Now we must hope that everything goes to plan and that Pug Banzinni will be recaptured.'

'Of course he will,' Kevin said. And on that positive note they ended their discussion.

That night they lay awake thinking of the events

which would unfold on Friday. If everything went to plan they would prevent the escape of a very dangerous criminal. But if anything went wrong with their plan then no one could say what might happen. They remembered what had happened to Kevin. On Friday, they could be in even greater danger. It was a most disquieting thought.

# *14*

## THE PLOT UNFOLDS

The next morning the Dolans and Alan set off for the bog. As they approached the road leading to the airport, they saw an old man coming towards them. He was pushing a black bicycle which was as high as a farm gate and had great curled handlebars.

'It's Johnny Murphy,' David said. 'He must be going into Charlestown.'

'Well,' Johnny said. 'It's a grand day we're having.'

They agreed it was. 'A bit on the hot side,' Johnny went on. He wiped the sweat from his furrowed brow on the sleeve of the heavy coat he wore. It was a long coat and the hem clutched at his ankles when he walked. It was more suited to the winter as was the knitted hat he wore. But Johnny was never without either hat or coat, winter or summer.

'Ye're off to the bog, are ye?' Johnny asked.

'We are,' David said.

'Ye want to be minding the fairies then,' Johnny said. 'There's fierce numbers of them about these days. They do be sitting on the end of my bed at night, grinning up at me.'

'Oh, we'll be careful,' David said. He frowned at Alan, who was on the point of bursting out laughing.

'Do that,' Johnny said. 'Do that. And mind the ghosts and goblins too. Come here till I tell ye now.' He beckoned them with a knurled finger. 'I saw a ghost last night, so I did. Driving a hearse with a coffin in it. At midnight it was. A dangerous hour is midnight. The witches do be out flying on their broomsticks then. Many's the night I've seen their black shapes flying across the face of the moon. Tell me now,' he added, 'did ye ever see a witch?'

'No,' David said. 'I never saw one. But where was this ghost you saw driving the hearse? Where was he going?'

'He went into Mrs Kelly's cottage,' Johnny said. 'An American ghost it was. I heard him talking and swearing. I had to wash out my ears afterwards. Terrible strange goings on if you ask me.' Johnny scratched his stubbly face and seemed to go off into a world of his own. Without another word he moved on, pushing the bicycle.

As he moved off Alan nudged David. 'Who is he?' he asked. 'Is he mad or what?'

'He's known as Moonshiner,' David explained. 'He used to make poitín once. That's an illegal alcoholic drink distilled from barley. Apparently he had a liking for it himself and went a bit funny. But he's harmless. He's always talking about seeing fairies and ghosts and that. But I don't think it was an American ghost he saw last night going to Mrs Kelly's cottage. Do you?'

'Definitely not,' replied Alan. 'So now we know for certain that the hearse is at the cottage. One part of the plan to free Pug Banzinni has fallen into place.'

While the Dolans were on their way to the bog, Marian Mulligan set off for her first role as a movie star. She was terribly excited. A limousine took her to a great mansion outside Dublin, set in its own grounds. There Scarface Moran, who was pretending to be the movie's director, explained that she would spend the afternoon in rehearsals.

She had to act the part of a young girl who has been kidnapped and is being held for ransom. She was bound with strong rope and acted the part of the frightened victim. Moran was delighted with her performance and had a photographer take dozens of photographs.

'It's absolutely perfect,' he said. 'You're a born actress. Now, we'll start filming tomorrow. I have to return to Dublin but you will remain here tonight. We want to get an early start in the morning.'

Marian was thrilled and wanted to telephone her father with the good news.

'I'm afraid you can't,' Moran said. 'The picture is top secret. We don't want anyone to know you're here. I'm sure you understand.'

Marian did understand. She didn't want to jeopardise her career. When she was starting out, she felt it was best if she agreed with whatever the director wanted. But when she was a famous movie star she would insist on having what she wanted.

She had the evening to herself and went for a walk in the grounds. She strolled down to the main gate but was prevented from going any further by a tough-looking character with a broken nose.

'Can't let no one through.' He spoke out of the corner of his mouth. 'The Boss has given me orders.'

'Oh I see,' Marian said. She turned and went back to the house. It was obvious they couldn't allow her out for the same reason they couldn't allow her to use the telephone. They didn't want anyone to know she was here. She felt like a famous movie star already.

While Marian walked in the grounds a car sped towards Dublin. In the rear seat sat the photographer who had taken the pictures. Beside him lay his equipment case and rolls of film.

When the car reached the city the driver drove to a dingy house in the suburbs. Here the photographer got out and took his equipment and rolls of film inside. He went to a room with blackout curtains on the window. In the room there was photographic developing and printing equipment. He set to work to develop the films. The red light, which was the only illumination in the room, gave his pale, pinched face a ruddy complexion.

Soon he had the films developed and checked the negatives with a practised eye. He chose two dozen negatives for printing. In each of them Marian looked terrified. He printed the negatives and when they were dry he checked them and was well pleased with his work. He was an expert at his job, one of the best in the city. But very few people knew of his existence. All his work was for criminals.

He left the dark room and found himself blinking as the bright light struck his eyes. He went to the telephone in the hall and dialled a number. Scarface Moran, who was now back in Dublin, answered.

'The photographs are ready,' the photographer said. 'I think you'll be pleased with my work.'

'I'd better be,' Moran threatened. 'I'm coming now to collect them.'

'Just make sure you bring the money,' the photographer added.

'I'll have the money,' Moran said and hung up.

The photographer returned to his dark room. He checked the photographs again and put them in a wallet. They were of excellent quality and Moran would be pleased. They would certainly do the job – whatever job he intended to do with them.

Moran soon arrived to collect the photographs. The photographer handed them over and was paid for his work. Later Moran and his trusted henchman, Hal, examined the photographs.

'They're perfect, Boss,' Hal said.

'Couldn't be better,' Moran agreed. 'I think they'll convince Captain Mulligan all right. We won't have any problem with him.'

'We won't fail,' Hal said. 'But will Slim and Tiny be able to deal with their part of the plan?'

'They had better be able,' Moran said. 'If they fail, then our plan will fail. If that happens it'll be concrete socks for everyone.'

That evening a limousine approached Charlestown. The driver had a map on the seat beside him and he looked at it as he came into the town. Satisfied he had the right directions, he drove through the town and took the Swinford Road. Outside the town he turned left on to a narrow tarred road. He drove on and soon saw Knock Airport in the distance. He was almost there.

Now he rapped on the partition separating the cab from the body of the vehicle. It was the prearranged signal he had agreed with his passenger when they left Dublin three hours before.

The limousine passed the road leading to the airport and swung into a series of tight bends. Just then it met a herd of cows being driven by a farmer. Behind the farmer there was a boy and a girl driving a pony and cart.

The limousine stopped. The driver tapped impatiently on the steering wheel while the dumb animals shuffled with agonising slowness past his window. At last they passed by and the farmer raised his hand in greeting.

The passenger was puzzled by the unexpected delay. He thought he might have reached his destination and the driver had forgotten to signal to him. Curious as to where he was, he pulled across a corner of the curtain on the side window of the limousine. He had been strictly forbidden to look out at any time on the journey but who would know? He only wanted a little peep.

At the moment he pulled the curtain aside, the pony and cart was just passing. The boy and girl stared at him and he couldn't help but note the look of amazement which crossed their faces. Their disbelieving eyes were locked to his for a moment and then he saw fear replace the disbelief.

He couldn't understand that. Why would they be frightened? Was there something wrong with his face? He knew that the make-up had altered his appearance but he still didn't think he looked that frightening. He thought he might ask the driver or the men he would meet at the cottage why the children should be frightened of him. But then they would know he had disobeyed orders and would be angry. It might be best to remain silent. He let the curtain drop into place and sat back in his seat as the limousine moved forward again.

As it drove on Cathy Dolan stopped the pony and she and Kevin stared after the limousine. They never took their eyes from it until it turned left and disappeared from view, heading towards Mrs Kelly's cottage. Only then did they turn to look at each other, fear still visible on their faces.

'Don't worry, Kevin,' Cathy said. 'It's not him. He's still in prison.'

'Maybe he's escaped already,' Kevin said, a tremor in his voice.

'No, he hasn't,' Cathy said firmly. 'We know exactly who that is in the limousine.' Despite the conviction in her voice, she turned away and closed her eyes to try and clear the image from her mind. But it persisted. She could still see the face peering out at her. It was that face she had seen on the newspaper – the cruel, toothless face of Pug Banzinni.

## 15

## ACTION DAY

At dawn on Friday morning David and Alan hid their bicycles a quarter of a mile from the cottage. Then they scampered across the fields and approached the cottage from the rear. When they were within 100 yards of it they crouched behind a stone wall and observed the cottage. All the curtains were drawn. There was no sign of life. They kept watch until they were satisfied that no guard was posted.

'I'd best go in,' Alan whispered eventually. 'There's no knowing when they might get up.'

David nodded. 'Go on, then,' he urged. 'I'll keep watch. If I give a shrill whistle, then get out of there as fast as you can.'

'OK,' Alan nodded, his face tense. As he clambered over the low stone wall David crossed his fingers for luck.

With the key in his pocket, along with a torch and pliers, and carrying a basin he had borrowed from Mary Dolan's kitchen, Alan scampered towards the large shed. When he reached it he leaned against the side of the shed, out of sight of the cottage. He was breathing hard and his heart was pounding.

After a moment he held his breath and listened. The breeze rustled the hedge. Nearby, some birds sang. In the distance a cow lowed. But there was no sign of danger. He crept along the side of the shed and peered around the corner. All was clear. Boldly he stepped out and moved to the door.

Quickly Alan unlocked the door and opened it. The hinges were unoiled and squeaked loudly in protest. In the silence Alan was certain that the noise could be heard miles away. He stopped and held his breath, listening intently. But no warning whistle came.

He entered the shed and saw the hearse containing the coffin right there before him. He sucked in his breath and shuddered. The urge to flee gripped him but he clenched his fists and fought it. Everything depended on him just now. He couldn't let the others down.

He knew that while he was in the shed he was in grave

danger. If Slim or Tiny or one of the other thugs who must now be here at the cottage were to come along he was trapped. He thought of Kevin and the ordeal he had suffered, and shivered. But he thrust his fear away. He had to concentrate on the job in hand.

Alan took out his torch and pliers and lay on the floor. He inched his way under the front of the hearse. He switched on the torch and shone it upwards. Immediately he saw the drain tap for the radiator. He took the pliers and gripped the tap in the jaws. He twisted the pliers but nothing happened. Again and again he tried but the tap was stuck fast.

Breathing heavily, he grabbed the pliers with both hands and gave a terrific twist. With a creaking sound, not unlike that made by the door hinges, the tap moved a fraction. Two more twists eased the tap fully.

Alan now carefully positioned the basin and twisted the tap with his fingers. Water dribbled out and then flowed freely. The noise it made seemed to Alan's ears like that of a river in full flow. But he knew that it was his heightened tension that made it seem so.

When the basin was almost full, Alan turned off the tap and inched his way back out from under the hearse. He checked that all was clear before venturing out with the basin. He disposed of the dirty brown water under the hedge and returned to the shed and went through the procedure again. This time, when he had almost filled the basin, he shut off the tap tightly and, on leaving the shed, relocked the door.

He disposed of the water again and made his way to where David waited.

'Mission accomplished,' Alan said. 'Now, let's hope they don't check the hearse for water.'

'If they do,' David said, 'there's little we can do about it. We can only hope that everything goes to plan.'

Alan nodded. 'Let's go,' he said. 'I'm starved and well ready for my breakfast.'

That same morning Marian Mulligan awoke early. She dreamed that night that she saw her name written up in sparkling lights in Hollywood. The dream had excited her and, immediately she awoke, she leapt out of bed. She dressed quickly and rushed downstairs, eager to have breakfast and start filming.

The great house seemed hushed around her. She went into the dining room and saw there was only one place set for breakfast. It was all most odd.

Just then she heard a noise and swung around. The man she had met at the main gate yesterday entered the room.

'My wife will get you breakfast soon,' he said.

'Where's everyone?' Marian asked.

'They haven't come from Dublin yet,' the man explained.

Marian nodded and sat at the table. After some minutes the middle-aged woman who'd served the meals yesterday brought in the breakfast. Marian was young and healthy and tucked into the wholesome food. She ate everything and drank two cups of coffee. Then the woman cleared the table. Marian tried to talk with her but the woman gave her a surly look and stalked back to the kitchen.

Marian stretched and yawned. All that food had made her feel lazy. She yawned again and decided that the excitement had been too much for her. She was tired and a little sleepy. Maybe a lie down would do her some good. She didn't want to be tired when the director returned to begin filming.

Marian made her way back upstairs to her room. Already her feet felt as if they were made of lead and her eyelids were drooping under their own weight. She stumbled to the bed and threw herself down on it. Even as she stretched out on the bedspread, sleep claimed her.

A minute later the middle-aged woman entered the room. She crossed to the bed and carefully lifted one of

Marian's eyelids. A blank eye stared up at her. Satisfied with what she saw, the woman left the room.

Downstairs her husband was waiting at the front door. 'Well?' he asked.

'The sleeping pills I put in her coffee have worked,' the woman said. 'She will sleep for most of the day. By the time she awakes Pug Banzinni will have escaped.'

'Let's get out of here so,' the man said. Both of them left the house, closing the door behind them. They got into a car which was parked outside and drove away. They didn't look back once.

After their own breakfasts that same morning the Dolans and Alan left for the bog. David drove the pony and cart while Cathy and Alan took their bicycles. They had the walkie-talkies and Thomas Dolan's binoculars with them. The early morning had been quite chilly but now the sun was high in a cloudless sky.

'I'd hate to be Pug Banzinni later today,' David said. 'He'll find it hot where he's going.'

'Not as hot as it'll be when the gardai arrest him,' Cathy said, and they laughed. But despite the laughter they were apprehensive. It would be hours yet before anything happened. They didn't know how they were going to pass the time until then.

Once on the bog they threw themselves into the work. They decided that keeping busy was the best way to make the hours fly. But their watches counted down the hours and the minutes agonisingly slowly.

They stopped for a break and later for lunch. But they ate little. For once the bog hadn't given them an appetite. After lunch they returned to work but now they were growing even more tense as the watches counted down the minutes one by one. Alan had a very elaborate watch with an alarm which he had set for half-past two. Now at last it bleeped. It was the signal for action.

'This is it,' David whispered as they huddled together. 'Each of us knows what to do. Cathy goes to the Garda station. Alan will watch the airport and runway to ensure that the Americans don't change the plan at the last moment. We don't want the gardai to go chasing the wrong Pug Banzinni. Kevin and I will drive the pony and cart out to the stack of turf at the roadside. From there we can watch the road to the cottage. Now, are there any questions?' But there were no questions. They had been over the details so often they each knew exactly what had to be done.

Cathy left immediately for Swinford Garda station. She took with her the details of the route marked on the map.

David had noted the registration numbers of the

hearse and the two limousines at the cottage.

At three o'clock Alan set off for the airport, taking with him one of the walkie-talkies and the binoculars. David kept the other walkie-talkie with him. As soon as Alan had gone, David and Kevin drove the pony and cart out to the roadside. Everything was now set.

# 16

## PUG GOES FLYING

Pug Banzinni was taken from the prison in a black van, its windows covered with steel grills. Two detectives sat with him as the van sped through the countryside. All three were silent. Two gardai on motorcycles, with blue lights flashing, led the way. Behind them came a Garda car. The gardai were taking no chances. Pug noted the precautions and smiled to himself. Little did they know that soon he would be free and they would be chasing shadows.

The van took the turn for Shannon Airport off the Limerick-Galway road. Overhead a jet roared into the blue sky, speeding on its way to some far-off country. Along the approach road some old aircraft stood forlorn behind the wire fence. Once great monarchs of the air, they were now rusting hulks, abandoned and forgotten.

At the airport itself the van drove straight out on to the tarmac where a jumbo jet stood waiting like a great metal bird. There were officials from customs and emigration waiting to make the necessary checks. Once everything was in order Pug Banzinni was handed over to two American detectives. They were young and mean looking, with short cropped hair.

'Don't I get to buy some duty-free?' Pug complained. 'I'd like some cigars for my flight.'

'Just shaddap,' one of the American detectives growled. He grabbed Pug's arm while his companion grabbed the other arm. They frog-marched Pug on to the plane. They had been allocated three seats half way down the cabin. With a detective on either side of him, Pug sat down and fastened his seat belt.

The other passengers began to board. Few took notice of the three men sitting together. They assumed they were businessmen returning to New York. But there were two men who did take notice of the three passengers.

Scarface Moran and Hal boarded the plane just before take off. They sat in a row of seats just yards from the entrance to the flight deck. They had been the first passengers to check in at the departure desk and had asked for these seats. Now they fastened their seatbelts as the aircraft taxied out on to the runway.

On the flight deck Captain Mulligan and his crew made their final checks. It was purely routine. Everything was ready and now they waited for clearance for take off from the control tower.

Captain Mulligan opened the throttles. The aircraft began to vibrate under the thrust of the four great aero-engines. As he increased power the engine noise became a shrill scream. Now the whole aircraft seemed to strain under the enormous thrust which tried to propel it forward against the brake pressure.

Captain Mulligan and his co-pilot stared at the array of instruments before them. Slowly the gauges began to register. When sufficient thrust was achieved, Captain Mulligan released the brakes. The great engines sent the aircraft hurtling down the runway. Rapidly it gathered speed. Faster and faster it sped. The runway became a blur. Captain Mulligan watched his speed gauge. He was waiting for the exact moment when airspeed was attained. The gauge crept close to the mark. Then it seemed to hover for ages just short of it. Tension on the flight deck mounted. The gauge registered airspeed. Carefully and precisely Captain Mulligan operated his controls.

Slowly and ponderously and yet graceful as a great

bird, the jumbo jet lifted off from the runway. With a thunderous roar, the engines thrust the aircraft up into the blue sky at great speed.

In the tilted cabin Pug Banzinni leaned across the detective beside him and looked out the window. He saw the Irish countryside fall away below him, green fields and trees and houses and a river, and somewhere off to his left cars speeding along a road.

'Take a good look,' the detective said. 'You won't be seeing Ireland ever again.'

Pug didn't speak. Instead he smiled. If only the detective knew that in half an hour's time he would be a free man. The thought made Pug feel good. In fact, it was the best he had felt since being put in prison months before.

As the aircraft took off a man rushed to a telephone in the departure lounge at Shannon and dialled a number. A moment later a telephone rang on the desk of the manager of Knock Airport.

'Excuse me, gentlemen,' he said to the two American filmmakers who were sitting on the other side of the desk. He picked up the telephone and listened. Then he glanced at the two men.

'It's for you,' he said. 'That message you've been waiting for.'

Slim took the receiver. He listened a moment, nodded

with satisfaction, and handed the receiver back to the manager.

'Everything's fine,' he said, turning to Tiny, a huge smile on his face. 'The Boss is on his way.'

'Why, that's just fi—' The manager stopped speaking in mid-sentence and stared in horror. Tiny had produced a pistol from his pocket. It was pointing at the manager's chest. From across the desk the muzzle of the gun seemed like a great, black tunnel.

'Easy now,' Slim said quietly. 'We just need your assistance for a little while.'

'You're ... you're not making a film,' the manager stammered. 'You're robbers. But there's nothing of value here.'

'We won't steal anything,' Slim said. 'We just want to borrow your runway for a little while. Now, we'll go up to the control tower. Don't do anything silly. Don't try to warn anyone or make a signal.'

The manager knew it was pointless to refuse. He rose from behind his desk and led the way up to the control tower. Once there the Americans were soon in complete charge. Tiny kept his gun trained on the manager. Meanwhile, Slim produced a second gun which he kept trained on the control tower staff.

'Just do as you're told,' he said, 'and no one'll get hurt.

I want the runway cleared for an emergency landing. But under no circumstances are the emergency services to be alerted. We don't want them getting in our way. Now we've just gotta wait a little while for a signal on the radio.' He backed against the door to the tower which he had locked on entering and watched everyone, his ears attuned for the signal on the radio which would tell him that Pug Banzinni was on his way to Knock.

The jumbo jet was still climbing when Moran glanced at Hal and nodded. Hal rang the bell for the stewardess while Moran opened the thick paperback book he had in his lap. The centre of the pages had been cut out and in the recess sat a tiny gun. It was made entirely of plastic and because of this it hadn't triggered off the alarms at the point where passengers were checked before boarding. The gun didn't work but it was very realistic. Moran removed it from its hiding place and concealed it in the palm of his hand.

Within a few moments the stewardess came to see what Hal wanted. He spoke in a low voice and she had to lean across Moran in order to hear him. Slowly Moran opened his hand so that the stewardess saw the gun. At the same time he grabbed her arm.

'Don't scream or make a signal,' he warned, 'and you won't get hurt. I just want to speak with the Captain.

You're going to take me up to the flight deck. Do it now and keep smiling. I'll be right behind you with the gun.'

The stewardess was too frightened to do other than what she was told. She turned to face the flight deck and Moran rose from his seat. He had the gun concealed in his palm. The stewardess walked to the flight deck door and knocked and entered. Moran followed, closing the door behind him.

'What the ...?' Captain Mulligan asked, swivelling his head around. 'No passengers are allowed on the flight deck without permission.'

'Perhaps you will grant me permission, Captain.' Moran pointed the gun at Captain Mulligan as he spoke. 'Don't do anything stupid. Otherwise you will get hurt. I have other friends on board,' he lied, 'and they are also armed. We just want to take over your aircraft for a little while.'

'Hijackers,' Captain Mulligan said angrily. 'Pirates of the air. I'm not handing over my aircraft to you.'

'No,' Moran said quietly. 'Well, perhaps you would like to look at these photographs, Captain. Your daughter is decidedly beautiful, is she not?' He produced a number of photographs from his pocket and handed them to Captain Mulligan.

Captain Mulligan took the photographs and stared at the first one in horror. It was a picture of Marian. The same fear and horror he was experiencing was visible on her face. Strong ropes bound her tightly to the chair she was sitting on. Sick with apprehension Captain Mulligan looked through the remainder of the photographs. All were similar.

'She ... she wasn't making a film at all,' he mumbled.

'I'm afraid not, Captain,' Moran said. 'But no harm will come to her if you co-operate with us. If you don't co-operate I cannot guarantee her safety.' He let the threat sink in.

Captain Mulligan had to admit defeat. He was not afraid of the gun but he was terrified of anything happening to Marian. If he didn't do as this man wished, he might never see her again.

'I'll do whatever you want,' he said. 'But I must have your assurances that none of my passengers will be hurt.'

'I can assure you of that, Captain,' Moran said. 'It is not our intention to hurt anyone. You do as I tell you and in half an hour we will be gone. You and your aircraft will then be free to travel on.'

'But without a certain passenger,' Captain Mulligan thought. He knew Pug Banzinni was on board and guessed that what was happening was part of an attempt to free him. But there was little he could do about it. While these men held his daughter prisoner he was helpless.

'Now, Captain,' Moran said, 'would you be so kind as to contact the control tower at Knock Airport. This is the frequency you must use. Tell them you have an emergency, and that you wish to obtain permission to land. I think in the circumstances it will be granted.'

Captain Mulligan thought about defying the man and refusing to carry out his order. But then he remembered Marian, who looked so much like her mother. He nodded quietly and reached for the controls on the radio.

# 17

# THE GARDA STATION

Cathy Dolan cycled through Barnacougue and on towards Kilbride. It was hot but despite this she made good progress. She would be in plenty of time to warn the gardai. But as she approached Kilbride and saw the mobile phone mast on the hill, disaster struck. The bicycle began to shake and rattle and she knew she had a flat tyre.

She stopped to look and saw immediately that it was the front tyre. She looked at her watch. It was almost three and the aircraft carrying Pug Banzinni would soon be taking off from Shannon Airport. Filled with a sense of urgency, she propped the bicycle against the roadside wall and took her pump from the frame.

Growing breathless both from exertion and anxiety,

she inflated the tyre. Then, holding the pump in her hand, she leaped on the bicycle and shot off as fast as she could pedal. But it was hopeless. She had only gone a few hundred yards before the tyre went flat again.

She dismounted once more and in frustration struck the handlebars with the pump. She knew there was no point inflating the tyre again. She would only get another few hundred yards before it went flat once more. She turned to stare back down the road but there was no sign of any car coming along. Neither was there any house in the vicinity where she could get help.

Growing more desperate, she began to run forward, pushing the bicycle. It was uphill now and the heat and the exertion took their toll on her. Her lungs felt constricted and her heart was thumping like a great engine. On and on she ran, blind to everything except the need to reach the Garda station on time.

She saw a house ahead and somehow managed to quicken her pace. When she reached it she dashed through the gate and up the drive. Throwing the bicycle against the hedge she rushed to the front door and frantically banged on the wood. An old woman, clearly showing her surprise, answered the door and Cathy explained to her about the puncture.

'I have to warn the gardai urgently,' she gasped. 'My

brothers and cousin may be in terrible danger. Do you have a telephone I could use?'

The woman shook her head and Cathy clenched her fists.

'Do you have a bicycle I could borrow?' she asked. 'Oh, please. I must get to the Garda station.'

'There is a bicycle in the shed at the back of the house,' the woman said. 'It belonged to my grandson. You can borrow that.'

'Thanks,' Cathy blurted out, turning away and racing around the side of the house to the shed. She opened the door and saw the bicycle inside. It was an old BMX and appeared to be in good working order.

Cathy dragged the bicycle outside and immediately leaped on. She swept down the drive and through the gateway. Pedalling furiously, she soon reached the top of the hill and freewheeled down to the main road.

She swept through the town of Swinford and on to the Garda station on the far edge of the town. She propped the bicycle against the steps leading up to the entrance and stood a moment to get her breath back. But a glance at her watch showed her that it was twenty-five past three. Pug Banzinni's flight had taken off nearly half an hour ago.

With her heart thumping like a drum, she ran into the

Garda station. There was one garda in the reception area behind a glass screen. He glanced up and then continued writing on a pink form. Cathy banged on the glass.

'Excuse me,' she called. 'Excuse me.'

The garda glanced up again and she beckoned him frantically with her hand.

'Please hurry,' she urged. 'We don't have much time.'

The garda quickly got up and came across to her. 'Now then,' he said. 'What can I do for you?'

'There's a hijacking taking place at Knock Airport,' Cathy blurted out. 'The plane carrying Pug Banzinni to New York will be landing there any minute now. You must go there quickly or he will get away. Oh, please,' she added when she saw the garda was not taking her seriously. 'My brothers and cousin may be in terrible danger. I got a puncture and was delayed getting here. I had to take this boy's bicycle from a shed and ...'

'Stolen a bicycle, have you?' the garda asked sternly.

'No!' Cathy gripped the edge of the counter. 'There is a hijacking taking place at Knock Airport. You must try and stop it.'

'Really,' the garda said. 'A hijacking at Knock?' He didn't appear terribly interested or impressed.

Cathy was growing more and more desperate.

'Please believe me,' she pleaded. 'We taped the plan.

They have a helicopter and a hearse. They're using a decoy and while you're chasing him, the real Pug Banzinni will get away.'

At this the garda laughed. 'Now, now,' he said. 'That's enough of that sort of talk. Don't you know it's a serious offence to waste garda time? I'll make an exception for the hot day that's in it. We'll say the sun has gone to your head. Off home with you now. Give the boy back his bicycle and we'll say no more about it.'

'No!' Cathy said, frantic now. She glanced at her watch. The minute hand seemed to be moving before her very eyes. It was half-past three. The plane would have already landed. Pug Banzinni was probably on his way to the cottage right now.

What would the boys do when they realised the gardai weren't coming? Would they attempt to stop Pug Banzinni all by themselves? Cathy knew David only too well. It was exactly what he would do. By now Pug's henchmen would be everywhere. They would have guns and would be desperate. There was no knowing what might happen.

Cathy knew she had to do something to make the garda take notice. But what? Every second counted. The longer she delayed, the more dangerous it became for the boys. She stared around and saw a large potted plant in a corner of the reception area. She raced over to it and with a mighty heave, toppled it over.

'Hey!' the garda yelled, as the pot crashed to the floor. Elsewhere in the building someone called out. Suddenly people came running into the reception area from all directions. They gathered around and stared at Cathy in disbelief.

The garda in reception was trying to explain everything. Everyone was talking at once. Just then an older man arrived on the scene and the talk suddenly ceased.

'What's happening here?' he demanded. He looked around and his severe gaze alighted on Cathy. 'You,' he said. 'Did you do this?' He nodded at the overturned plant.

'Yes, sir,' Cathy said, shaking her clenched fists. 'I had to get your attention. My brothers and cousin are in grave danger. I was telling that garda all about it but he wouldn't believe me. We've got to hurry. Please, sir. There's no time to lose.'

'Is this true?' The older man turned to the garda in question.

'Yes, superintendent,' the garda said. 'I mean no, superintendent. She told me she stole a bicycle. Then she claimed there was a hijacking taking place at Knock Airport. Someone's supposed to be trying to escape. A Bug Pannini I think. It didn't make sense, sir.'

'Pug Banzinni,' Cathy screamed with frustration. 'He's the American criminal. His henchmen are trying to free him.'

'Banzinni?' The superintendent took a step nearer to Cathy. 'Did you say Pug Banzinni?' His eyes had narrowed and a nerve in his cheek began to twitch.

Cathy nodded, her whole body shaking. 'We taped their plan,' she said. 'His henchmen are hijacking his plane and forcing it to land at Knock.'

The superintendent nodded and suddenly became alert.

'We received a tip off,' he said, 'that an attempt would be made to free Pug Banzinni. But we thought that any such attempt would be made while he was in prison or on the way to the airport. So, that was all wrong. The attempt is being made right now under our very noses.'

He swung about and rattled off some orders. Gardai began to run in all directions.

'Come,' he said to Cathy, brusquely taking her arm. 'You can give us the details on the way.'

Accompanied by three other detectives in plain clothes, Cathy and the superintendent rushed outside to an unmarked car. Two of the gardai got into the front seats. Cathy and the superintendent and the other garda got into the rear seat. In a moment they were racing towards Knock Airport.

On the way Cathy told the whole story while the detective in the front seat operated a radio.

'You've been superb,' the superintendent enthused. 'Let's hope now that we're not too late. Anything on the radio, inspector?'

'The desk sergeant got through to the airport, sir,' the inspector said. 'He's confirmed that a flight from Shannon has landed there. They said it was due to technical problems.'

'That's it!' the superintendent exclaimed, unable to hide his excitement. 'We'll recapture Pug Banzinni yet. Is the back-up on the way?'

'Yes, sir,' the inspector said. 'We've also put an emergency plan into action. We're instructing all stations in the area to stand by to set up roadblocks. None of them will get away.'

'Excellent,' the superintendent smiled. 'Excellent. The spider is in the web. We must ensure he doesn't escape.'

Cathy sat, tensed, in the rear seat and stared out at the countryside which flashed past the window. Her nails dug into the palms of her hands. Her breath came in gulps and gasps and her heart was beating against her rib cage as if it wanted to escape from her body.

'Hang on, Cathy,' the superintendent said. 'We'll soon

be there. Your brothers and cousin will be safe then.'

Cathy nodded but fear still gripped her. What if they were too late? What if Pug Banzinni had got away already? She knew the boys would have tried to intervene when they realised the gardai were not going to get there on time. By now they might be in the hands of the criminals ... Cathy closed her eyes. She couldn't bear to think of what might be happening to them this very minute.

# 18

## PUG ESCAPES

Captain Mulligan knew it was pointless to oppose the men who had hijacked his aircraft. Now, his only concern was to land at Knock without incident. The safety of the passengers, his crew and the aircraft itself depended on him.

After he had spoken with air traffic control at Knock, Captain Mulligan was forced to make an announcement to his passengers. He informed them there was a technical problem with the aircraft and he would have to land at Knock. But there was no need to worry. They would land there shortly.

Captain Mulligan now had a flight path plotted for Knock Airport and turned his aircraft onto the new compass bearing. He was barely ten minutes away from landing.

Scarface Moran watched the crew and the panel of instruments on the flight deck. He knew little about aircraft and had to trust Captain Mulligan to follow instructions. Originally the plan had been simply to threaten the captain with the gun. But now Moran was glad that they had included the element of the threat to the captain's daughter. Captain Mulligan was a brave man and might have tried to trick them if he had not thought his daughter was in grave danger.

The jumbo jet began to descend and shuddered as the air brakes were applied. From the flight deck the countryside seemed to rise up towards the aircraft. There was a panoramic view of fields and lakes and bogland, the twisting snakes that were rivers and roads. Villages and towns loomed into view, along with farms and houses.

The aircraft dropped still lower. Its nose now pointed towards the runway which appeared ahead like a strip of black ribbon. Quickly the ribbon changed to a recognisable strip of tarmacadam. They were nearly there.

Captain Mulligan checked his instruments and gauges. All was normal. He reached out and flicked a switch. Outside, the undercarriage, with its giant black wheels, dropped down from the belly of the aircraft. They were ready now for touchdown.

The airport buildings loomed into view. But Captain

Mulligan hardly saw them. All his concentration was taken up with landing the aircraft safely. He held the control column gently but firmly as they swooped in low over the pine trees. He kept the nose up. There was a slight bump as the rear wheels touched down. The tyres screamed in protest. Smoke belched from the scorched rubber. Captain Mulligan eased the controls a fraction and the nose wheel dropped down on to the runway. They had landed.

Scarface Moran grabbed the rear of a seat to steady himself as the aircraft rapidly began to lose speed. He breathed a sigh of relief and wiped the sweat from his brow. His part of the plan was almost complete. Now it was up to the other members of the gang.

From his vantage point Alan watched the jumbo land through the binoculars. The deafening noise from the four jet engines rumbled across the countryside like thunder. He watched it swoop in low, its shadow darkening the ground. As it touched down, the helicopter, which had been circling the airport for the last five minutes, swooped down like a little bird following its mother to its nest.

Now Alan switched his attention to the limousine parked by the gate in the perimeter fence near the end of the runway. Two men sat in the front seats. Joey was driving. Bandy, so named because he had bandy legs like those of a cowboy, was in the passenger seat. The curtains on the rear windows were drawn. But Alan knew who was sitting inside.

As the aircraft landed, Bandy leapt from the limousine and opened the gate. The limousine drove through the gate and Bandy clambered back in. Spewing gravel from under its spinning tyres, the limousine raced up the track. It reached the runway just as the jumbo jet rolled to a stop. The limousine slewed round on the runway, tyres screaming, then sped along to stop under the giant nose of the aircraft.

Then the helicopter landed close by, and both Bandy and Joey scrambled from the limousine. They ran to the forward door of the aircraft. The door opened just then and Hal appeared in the opening. Bandy had a rope ladder which he threw up to Hal. The first time he missed but at the second attempt Hal caught the ladder.

There was a grappling iron attached to the ladder and Hal hooked it to a seat strut. Immediately, Joey and Bandy climbed up into the aircraft. As Hal helped them inside they drew guns from their pockets. The passengers were clearly frightened by now and Scarface, who was still on the flight deck, took over the intercom and made an announcement.

'Ladies and gentlemen,' he said. 'Do not panic. Everyone must remain seated. We want one passenger to come along with us. Then we will leave. Do not interfere with my men. Otherwise you will get hurt.'

As the announcement was made Hal moved down the aircraft to where Pug Banzinni sat. Hal had a gun in his hand.

'OK, Boss?' he asked. 'Shall we go?'

Banzinni nodded, grinning like a delighted garden gnome.

'I'm afraid I have to go, boys,' he laughed. 'I can't say it's been nice knowing you.' He unfastened his seat-belt and rose to his feet. The detective sitting in the aisle seat grabbed Pug's arm. But Hal nudged him with the gun barrel and the detective had to release his grip.

Still grinning all over his ugly face, Pug Banzinni swaggered down the aisle. Hal followed, backing all the way. The barrel of his gun never once wavered. When Pug reached the exit he shook hands with his two hench-men and with Scarface, who had come from the flight deck. Then Pug climbed down the ladder, followed by the other thugs. Hal waited behind to ensure no one tried to stop them.

Halfway down the cabin the two detectives stared from the window. But they couldn't see what was happening on the ground. All they could see was the helicopter. Only Alan had a bird's eye view of everything.

Through the binoculars, he watched Pug Banzinni step on to the ground. He was followed by Scarface, Bandy and Joey. Immediately Pug was bundled into the rear of the limousine. As Pug entered by one door the door opposite opened and a second Pug leapt out.

Alan watched the decoy run to the waiting helicopter. Anyone in the aircraft who was at a window could see the running figure and would assume that it was Pug Banzinni. As the decoy clambered into the helicopter, the rotors began to whirl faster. With a deafening roar the helicopter lifted into the sky. It tilted sideways, like a drunken bird, and sped southwards.

As the helicopter took off, Hal unhooked the grappling iron and threw the ladder to the ground. He jumped from the aircraft and Scarface and the other thugs broke his fall. All four scrambled into the limousine. A moment later it raced towards the gate in the perimeter fence.

On the aircraft the two American detectives scrambled into the aisle. But pandemonium had broken out. Passengers were shouting and jostling all around them. The detectives tried to shove their way towards the exit. But it was hopeless.

They tried to push past a very fat lady who was blocking the aisle. But she turned around furiously and began to hit them over the head with her handbag.

'Bullies,' she screeched. 'Thugs. Muggers.' Each of her words was emphasised by a blow of the handbag. The detectives retreated to their seats in the face of the onslaught, desperately trying to protect themselves with their hands and arms.

The assault brought a great cheer from some of the other passengers and the detectives blushed as red as tomatoes.

'Try and get the details of that helicopter,' one of them spluttered to his companion. 'Banzinni has escaped in it.' But the helicopter had already disappeared from view. The detectives exchanged furious looks through their raised arms. Pug Banzinni had got away and there was no one now to stop him.

'Ladies and gentlemen.' Captain Mulligan's quiet voice came over the intercom. 'Ladies and gentlemen,' he repeated, 'please resume your seats. The danger is now past. The hijackers have left the aircraft. When everyone is seated and wearing their seatbelts we will taxi back to the terminal.'

At this, the hubbub eased. Now the stewardesses went quietly among the passengers and gradually gained control of the situation. Soon everyone was seated again and wearing their seat-belts. A stewardess closed the door. A moment later the jumbo began to edge forward. It swung about and headed back to the terminal building.

Meanwhile, Alan watched the limousine as it sped out the gate. It swung left and raced away at high speed. He scanned the roads and listened for the sound of approaching sirens. But there were none. The gardai weren't coming. Something had gone terribly wrong.

Alan pressed the signal button on his walkie-talkie.

'Alan to David,' he said urgently. 'Do you read me? Over.'

'David here.' He heard David's excited voice. It seemed as if he was right beside him. 'Receiving you loud and clear. Over.'

'We have a serious problem,' Alan said. 'Help has not arrived. Vehicle with target is heading back towards base. I am coming to join you. It's up to you now. Do you understand? Over.'

'Message understood.' David's voice was strained by the tension. 'We will do everything we can. Please come quickly. Over and out.' He switched off the walkie-talkie and retracted the aerial. He looked anxiously at Kevin, who was holding his breath from the excitement.

'Pug Banzinni is heading this way, Kevin,' David said.

'The gardai haven't arrived yet. If we don't do something now to stop him, then he will get away. Are you ready to help me?'

Kevin was unable to speak. He merely nodded his head. The two brothers looked at each other. Their faces were drawn and pale. They were now in the most dangerous phase of the whole operation. And they were on their own. If anything went wrong now there was no one to help them.

# 19

## OUT FOR THE COUNT

Up in the control tower, Slim and Tiny also watched the drama unfold on the runway. They watched as the helicopter roared away and then they shook hands with each other.

'Well, there goes Pug Banzinni,' Slim said, winking at Tiny. 'He should be at Shannon Airport in half an hour. Just in time to catch a flight out of the country.'

'Our part in the operation has been a great success,' Tiny said.

They grinned at each other and continued to watch the runway until they saw the limousine roar safely away.

'We'd best be on our way,' Slim said now. 'Thanks very much for your hospitality,' he added to the manager and control tower staff. 'You've been most helpful.'

'Very obliging.' Tiny roared with laughter. He thought it was the best joke he had cracked in a long time.

'Have a nice day now,' Slim said. 'We're very sorry but we have to go. We'll just lock you in here for a little while. You can have a little party together to celebrate our success.'

The thugs laughed as they backed out of the tower and locked the door behind them. Once outside, their faces became serious. They dashed downstairs and rushed through the terminal building to the exit. The whole place seemed to be in turmoil. People were running hither and thither.

But Slim and Tiny ignored it all. They rushed out to their limousine and in a moment were roaring away at great speed. In half an hour they would rendezvous with the other thugs and then make their way to Dublin Airport. From there they would all take different flights to freedom.

As they made their escape, the airport manager was issuing commands to the staff in the control tower.

'Contact the authorities at Shannon Airport immediately,' he ordered the radio operator. 'Inform them that Pug Banzinni is on his way there by helicopter. He is going to try and leave the country. The gardai must be prepared to prevent him from doing so.'

'Yes, sir,' the radio operator said. He turned to his

radio and began to operate the dials. In a few moments he was speaking to the authorities at Shannon Airport.

While all this was happening, David and Kevin were anxiously awaiting the arrival of the limousine carrying the real Pug Banzinni.

'What can have happened to Cathy?' Kevin asked. 'The gardai should have been here by now if she told them about the hijacking.'

'I don't know what could have gone wrong,' David said. He stared back up the road, looking for any sign that the gardai were on their way. But all he could see was the limousine carrying Pug Banzinni speeding towards them.

'Pug's going to get away,' Kevin clamoured. 'What are we going to do?'

'We'll try and delay them,' David said. 'It's all we can do.'

The pony and cart had been pulled onto the grass verge. The pony was cropping the tasty grass, oblivious to what was happening. Now David drove the pony and cart onto the middle of the road, blocking the way. Soon the limousine roared up behind them. They heard the screech of the brakes as it was forced to stop. The horn blew stridently. Slowly both boys turned to look.

Hal had the front passenger's window wound down and his head stuck out the opening.

'Get that contraption out of the way,' he roared.

'Contraption?' David said. 'What's a contraption?'

'That ... that ...' Hal spluttered. 'Get it off the road.'

'The road is a bit narrow,' David said. 'I'll pull into the first gap I come to and let you pass.'

'Pull in now!' Hal's voice seemed to make the day go cold. Suddenly a gun appeared in his hand. It was pointing directly at David.

'Yes, sir,' David said. 'Right away.' He didn't have to pretend to be afraid. From yards away the gun looked as frighteningly large as a cannon. He pulled the pony and cart off the road and the limousine roared by in a whoosh of wind. It accelerated away, swaying on its springs.

David and Kevin stared at each other, then turned to look back in the direction from where the limousine had come. But there was still no sign of any other vehicle. Clearly the gardai were not coming.

Pug Banzinni could hardly believe things had gone so smoothly. At last, after months in prison, he was a free man. In a few hours he would be on board ship and in two days would land on the coast of Spain under cover of darkness. Using his false passport, he would return to America and wreak vengeance on the man who had caused him all the trouble.

Thinking of what he would do to this man put Pug

into an even better mood. He would give him the concrete sock treatment again. And just for good measure, he would make him a pair of concrete gloves too. That would keep his hands nice and warm for the winter.

At this Pug laughed.

'What's so funny, Boss?' Moran asked.

Pug explained his new idea. All the thugs chuckled. 'You could pull out all his teeth with a pliers,' Moran suggested.

'Pull out his toenails and fingernails,' Hal added.

'Cut out his tongue,' Bandy said. 'That would stop him talking.' At this they all laughed again and Pug thought it was good to be free. He could hardly wait to get back to robbing banks.

'Cottage coming up soon, Boss.' Moran, who sat beside Pug, now spoke and the laughter ceased. 'Everything's ready. It'll only take a moment to give you the drug and fit the disguise. Then we can put you in the coffin and you can head off for Mulranny.'

Pug shivered. It was the part of the plan he dreaded. When he reached the cottage he would put on a false beard and moustache. With this disguise, he would resemble the picture on the false passport. Then he would be given an injection which would paralyse him for at least half an hour. After that he would be placed in the coffin and taken by hearse to Mulranny.

The drug was necessary in case the hearse was stopped by the gardai. If they did stop it and check the coffin, they would think Pug was really a dead man. Of course, it was unlikely the gardai would suspect the hearse as a getaway vehicle. Especially when they learned that Pug Banzinni had escaped by helicopter. That was the other brilliant part of the scheme – to use a decoy to take the gardai off his trail.

The limousine reached the cottage and swung in through the gate. As it stopped, Speedy, who had remained behind at the cottage, opened the shed door. Pug, Moran and Bandy got out of the limousine. Moran carried a small case. They slipped into the shed and once they were inside, Speedy closed the door. He switched on a light he had wired up to a car battery, and the shed became as bright as day. He then climbed into the driver's seat of the hearse. The keys were in the ignition. Everything was ready.

Pug saw the rear door of the hearse was open and the lid of the coffin stood against the wall. He stared at both and trembled with fear. But there could be no turning back. If he hesitated now he would spend the rest of his life in prison.

Moran opened the case and removed the beard and moustache. He took a tube of spirit gum and liberally smeared it on both items. Then he carefully stuck the beard and the moustache on to Pug's chin and upper lip. He took a step back to admire his handiwork and nodded, well satisfied. No one would now think the man before him was Pug Banzinni.

Pug removed his jacket and rolled up his shirt sleeve. Moran took a hypodermic syringe and needle from the case and, grabbing Pug's arm, plunged the needle into the flesh. The master crook, the most feared criminal in America, gave a groan. His eyes rolled in his head and he slumped down in a heap on the floor. He had fainted and was out for the count.

Bandy laughed and Moran swung about furiously and struck him.

'Fool,' he snarled. 'This is no time for laughing. Help me get Pug into the coffin.'

But it was no easy task. Pug was very heavy. They huffed and puffed as they tried to lift him up into the hearse. But it was hopeless.

'Come and help us,' Moran ordered Speedy. 'We've no time to lose.'

With Speedy's help, they eventually managed to get Pug into the coffin, where they stretched him out. They placed his hands down by his sides. Moran made a final check to ensure Pug was breathing. He was, but with the paralysing drug now taking effect, he would pass for someone who was dead.

Speedy climbed back into the cab while Moran and Bandy put the lid on the coffin. Moran then checked the air holes which had been drilled in the coffin and were hidden by the handles. Satisfied that Pug wouldn't suffocate, Moran slammed down the rear door.

Speedy started the engine while Bandy opened the shed door. Already Joey had pulled the limousine aside to allow the hearse to drive out. Hal was out on the road and he gave the all-clear signal.

Speedy now gunned the engine and the vehicle surged forward. He swung out the gate on to the road and turned left. With a roar from the engine and a crash of gears he sped away.

Moran locked the door of the shed and he, Bandy and Hal leapt into the limousine. It sped off in the other direction, heading for the arranged rendezvous with Slim and Tiny. As they drove along, they dreamed of the money promised them by Pug Banzinni as a reward for their loyalty and services. Soon they would be very rich men.

## 20

# HEROES IN ACTION

Speedy was anxious to get away as quickly as possible and so he drove very fast. He had been warned not to speed as this might attract attention. But he was scared. It was all right for the others to talk. They didn't have Pug Banzinni lying in a coffin behind their backs.

From habit, Speedy stared at the array of gauges before him. But he wasn't at all worried. Last night he had thoroughly checked the vehicle and everything had been in order. The engine was running as smoothly as a sewing machine. Nothing could go wrong.

So it was with horror he noticed the temperature gauge creeping into the red. The engine was overheating. But that couldn't be. When he had checked the radiator for water last night it had been filled right to the brim. There was something wrong with the gauge, that was all.

Speedy breathed a sigh of relief. But his relief was short lived, for just then he noticed smoke curling from under the bonnet. Only it wasn't smoke. It was steam! He watched the wisp grow bigger as the hearse swerved around a bend in the road. Up ahead he saw a pony and cart being driven by two boys. It was blocking his way. Speedy slammed on the brakes and the hearse screeched to a halt.

Speedy opened the door and leaped out. He rushed to the front of the hearse and lifted up the bonnet. As he did so a cloud of steam belched out with a great whoosh. Speedy flailed his arms and in his black undertaker's suit and hat he looked like a large gentleman crow flying through a cloud.

He hurriedly hopped back, aware now that the radiator must be low in water. He couldn't figure out how that had happened. But he did know he was in serious trouble. By now the gardai would have been informed of what had occurred. They might be racing towards him at this very moment. He would be caught and put in prison for a long time.

He needed water. But it was much too far to go back to the cottage. He didn't have time. And there were no other houses around. Desperately he turned to the boys.

'I need water for the radiator,' he said. 'I need it urgently. Where can I get some?'

'I don't know,' David said. He stared at the hearse and the coffin. He couldn't believe that Pug Banzinni was in there. If he was to step forward and put out his hand he could touch the glass ... He turned to scan the road anxiously. But there was no sign of a Garda car. If he and Kevin didn't act right now, Pug would get away. If only they could delay the hearse a little longer. But what could they do?

Speedy let out a bellow like a frightened animal, rushed forward and grabbed David's shoulders.

'I need water,' he blabbed with fear. 'Where can I get some? Tell me, boy, or you'll be sorry.' He clenched his fist and raised it threateningly.

Up close, Speedy looked menacing. Kevin was scared he would hurt David.

'There,' Kevin said, pointing. 'You can get water in the bog hole.'

'That's right,' David said. 'Just there.' He pointed to the corner of the bog. 'There's a bog hole there filled with water. Just cross the heather and you'll reach it quickly.' He looked warningly at Kevin, who stayed quiet.

Speedy released David. 'Have you got a container?' he asked.

'Yes,' David said. He was co-operative now. He took a rucksack out of the cart. In it was the bottle containing the lemonade they had brought to the bog. He handed the bottle to Speedy.

Speedy was feeling a little better. He was pleased with himself. He had soon frightened this brat of a boy. There was nothing like the threat of violence to get whatever it was you wanted. He would get out of here yet. Overawed with his power, he shoved David out of his way. Then he strode off into the bog. Halfway along the passage he veered left.

Not daring to breathe, David and Kevin watched him. Speedy took two more steps and then suddenly disappeared from view with a yell of fear. He had fallen into the hidden drain.

The boys watched his hands scrabbling at the heather as he tried to get a grip. The black hat bobbed up and down, like a mole surfacing in a lawn. Slowly it reappeared. There was little water in the drain because of the dry summer so Speedy wasn't very wet. But they could tell from the way he glared back at them and waved his fists that he wasn't exactly happy with events.

The boys weren't exactly happy either. They had hoped to stop or at least slow down Speedy's progress. But he had been delayed by no more than fifteen or twenty seconds.

Now though, Speedy took more care as he moved forward. He inched his way along, picking his steps carefully until he reached the spot David had indicated. He tiptoed to the edge of the bank and looked over. Satisfied with what he saw, he went down on his knees and lowered the bottle into the water. When it was filled he began to rise up from his knees. It was then it happened.

Speedy was on the exact spot where the bank had been undermined by the weather. His weight was too much for the brittle ground and as he rose it broke away from under his feet. He yelled and threw up his hands. The bottle went flying through the air. He tried desperately to retrieve his balance, swaying backwards and forwards. But it was to no avail. With a scream of horror and a great splash, Speedy toppled head first into the water.

The bottom of the bog hole was muddy. Speedy's head sank into the mud to the depth of the brim of the hat. He became stuck there, with his legs flailing the air, as if he were riding a bicycle upside down. He gasped and swallowed water and mud. It was all sticky and slimy and tasted horrible. Mud went in his eyes and up his nose and in his ears. He was now blind and deaf and couldn't breathe.

Slowly, ever so slowly, he overbalanced. The hat remained stuck in the mud while Speedy's head came loose. He toppled over backwards with another splash and his head came clear of the water. He was now lying on his back, staring up sightlessly at the sky.

He lay there for a few moments gasping for breath and spitting out mud and water. Then he cleared the mud from his eyes and turned over and began to drag his soaking wet body from the bog hole. When he found himself on dry ground he lay, face down, for a moment and spat out the last of the mud. Then he remembered the predicament he was in and how he had come to be in it.

Revenge! The word loomed large in Speedy's brain. He forgot all about Pug Banzinni. He forgot about the gardai. Now he just wanted to catch and severely punish the two boys who had brought about his humiliation.

David and Kevin had been struck dumb as they watched Speedy struggle in the bog hole. They hadn't even dared to laugh. They were hoping that the gardai would arrive before Speedy got out of the bog hole and came to wreak vengeance on them. Just then they heard a noise behind them. Pug Banzinni had somehow got out of the coffin! He was creeping up on them right now! It was the one thought in their minds as they swung about in sheer terror. But to their utter relief, they saw it was only Alan arriving on the scene.

'The gardai still haven't come,' David said urgently. 'And we've only succeeded in delaying Speedy. We'll have to do something ourselves if Pug Banzinni isn't to escape. But we'll have to move fast. Now I've got an idea. Open the tailgate of the hearse, Alan. I'll bring the pony and cart around to the back. Quickly now. Speedy's just got out of the bog hole.'

'Right!' Alan exclaimed. Kevin gave a whoop of relief. They were going to do something at last.

While Alan opened the tailgate, David brought the pony and cart to the rear of the hearse. Quickly and skilfully, he reversed the cart in tight to the opening. Kevin took the pony's head and held him steady. Now, with Alan on one side and David on the other, they began to roll the coffin out on its rollers and into the cart.

Just then they heard a rattling noise. It came from the direction of the cottage. Some of the other thugs must be coming. They were trapped. They all stood as if frozen on the spot. Half the coffin was in the cart while the other half still remained in the hearse.

A moment later a figure on a bicycle sped round the bend. It was only Moonshiner. They watched him approach, his eyes and mouth opening wider and wider. He drew near, stopped the bicycle and dismounted. He stared at the hearse and the coffin and the boys and the pony and cart. Then he stared into the bog. Speedy was screaming and screeching and jumping up and down like a demented water rat.

'Oh,' Moonshiner moaned. 'Oh.' His face turned a deathly pale and his eyes bulged in their sockets. 'What's happening?' he mumbled. 'I'm seeing things. I'm going mad.'

'It's only me, Moonshiner,' David said.

'It speaks.' Moonshiner emitted a terrible moan. 'Oh, please help me. The world's gone mad. I won't touch another drop. No, never another drop. I swear it.'

'It's all right, Moonshiner,' David repeated, walking towards the old man. 'It's only me.'

At this, Moonshiner threw up his hands in horror. With no support, the bicycle fell with a clatter on the road. Moonshiner took to his heels and began to run back towards the cottage, his coat billowing about him.

Just then a blood-curdling bellow of rage came from the direction of the bog and again the boys swung around in horror. Speedy was flailing his arms in the air like a windmill in a storm. Water sprayed off him as it would from a wet dog shaking itself dry. With another blood-curdling bellow, he charged towards them.

The boys' hearts stopped beating for a moment. They gaped in awe at the rampaging figure of Speedy. It mesmerised them and they couldn't move. It was David who broke the spell.

'Come on, come on,' he urged. 'We've only got a few seconds.'

Alan didn't need urging. He and David grabbed the handles of the coffin again and began to shove it into the cart. It seemed to weight a ton at least, but their fear seemed to give them strength. Part of the coffin stuck out the back but they didn't have time to worry about that.

'Up on the cart, Kevin,' David commanded, fear and urgency in his voice. 'Drive like the wind.'

Kevin didn't hesitate. He leapt on to the cart and grabbed the reins. There was no time to lose. He cracked the reins and urged the pony forward.

'Gee up, Dobber,' he called. 'Gee up.'

Dobber seemed aware of the urgency and set off at a gallop. He skirted the fallen bicycle and quickened his pace. Kevin didn't dare to look behind him. He was terrified he would see Pug Banzinni leap from the coffin and grab him by the scruff of the neck.

As the cart pulled away, Alan raced for his bicycle. It was only then that David realised he had no means of escape. The cart was already 100 yards up the road and gathering speed. He would never catch it. At that moment Alan shot past him.

'Come on, come on,' Alan yelled. 'He's almost upon you.'

David was only too well aware of this. Speedy was

very close now. In another few seconds all would be lost. David took a last desperate glance towards the figure who was blindly thundering down on him and swung back. He saw Moonshiner's bicycle lying in the centre of the road and didn't hesitate for a second. He raced to the bicycle, picked it up and leaped on. He began to push the pedals with all his might while behind him, Speedy drew nearer. David could now hear his laboured breathing and he made a greater effort. But it wasn't enough. At that very moment Speedy grabbed his T-shirt.

Speedy's grip tightened.

'Stop,' he roared, seemingly in David's ear. Fear gave David the urge to pedal harder. But it was to no avail. Slowly but surely Speedy began to haul him back.

'Keep going,' David shouted at Alan, who was up ahead. 'Save yourself. Get away.' But Alan ignored David's shouts. Instead he swung his bicycle around and came back towards them. When he drew level with them he lashed out at Speedy with his foot. His first kick missed but the second caught Speedy in the side and he gasped with pain. A moment later, David felt Speedy's fingers release their grip. He was free.

He sped away and was soon joined by Alan. As they raced round the bend in the road they saw Kevin up ahead with the cart. Off to their right they caught a glimpse of Moonshiner. He was running across the fields as if all the goblins in the world were chasing him.

David and Alan eased off pedalling and looked at each other. They were exhausted from the effort and the tension. But they were also triumphant. They took their hands from the handlebars of their bicycles and clenched their fists in the air, giving a great victory roar.

They caught up with Kevin and, after praising him, they discussed what they should do now. Kevin suggested they conceal the pony and cart and the coffin in the large shed at the cottage.

'No one will ever think of looking there,' he said.

David and Alan agreed it was an excellent idea. They continued on to the cottage and Alan, who still had the key for the padlock in his pocket since the morning, soon had the doors open. Kevin drove Dobber into the shed and whispered some words of praise in the pony's ear. David and Alan also concealed the bicycles in the shed and Alan then relocked the door.

The three climbed into the field next to the cottage and hid behind the stone wall to await developments. But whatever happened now, they knew Pug Banzinni would not escape again.

## 21

## THE GARDAI ARRIVE

When Speedy got his breath back, his only thought was to get away. Pug Banzinni would have to look out for himself. Speedy turned and ran back to the hearse, holding his aching ribs with one hand at the spot where Alan had kicked him. He intended to drive the hearse as it was. He might get a few miles on before the engine seized up.

As he ran, the water squelched in his shoes and he left a wet trail on the road. He was soaked from head to foot and bits of green slime clung to his clothes and his hair. His ears were filled with mud and he prised some of it out with a finger as he ran. Just as he reached the hearse he heard the noise of an approaching car. Quickly he ducked down at the side of the hearse and watched from there. He didn't want to be seen if a Garda car came along.

The car approached. It was unmarked and as it drew near Speedy saw it contained five passengers, four men and a young girl. Obviously it wasn't a Garda car. It posed no danger to him and he decided he would try and get a lift. He emerged from beside the hearse and waved his hand. The car stopped and one of the passengers, wound down the rear side window.

'My hearse has broken down,' Speedy explained. 'I need help.'

'Have you been swimming?' the superintendent asked, for it was the gardai who had arrived at last. At this the others in the car laughed.

This angered Speedy but he held his temper. He desperately needed help and this might be his only chance of getting some.

'I was getting water from a bog hole,' he explained, 'and I fell in. Now I need a lift to the nearest town. Could you take me?'

'Certainly not,' the superintendent said. 'We can't allow a wet duck in here. You would ruin my upholstery. But my two friends are experts on engines. They will see what they can do for you.'

Speedy wished he had a gun. Then he would teach these fools a lesson. But he had been forbidden to carry any weapon in case he was stopped by the gardai and searched. Now all he could do was accept whatever help these persons might give him. If he could get water for the radiator he could make his escape.

Two of the detectives got out of the car. They asked Speedy to show them what was wrong with the engine. Speedy walked over to the hearse and stooped down to point into the engine. As he did so the detectives grabbed him and snapped handcuffs on his wrists.

The superintendent got out of the car. 'Now then,' he said, 'tell us where Pug Banzinni is?'

'Never heard of him,' Speedy growled.

'Please yourself,' the superintendent said. 'But each minute you stay silent will mean more time in prison. I'll see to that personally.'

'OK,' Speedy said. 'What do you want to know?'

'We want Banzinni,' the superintendent explained. 'We know you're trying to help him escape. But it seems to me you've been careless and gone and lost him.'

'It was these boys,' Speedy said angrily. 'They've kid-napped him. They had this pony and cart and they sent me into the bog for water. Only I fell in the bog hole and got all wet. While I was trying to get out of the hole they took the coffin away in the cart. They went that way.' He pointed back towards the cottage.

'It's them,' Cathy shouted from the car. She could hardly hide her excitement. 'They've got Pug Banzinni. I knew they wouldn't let us down.'

'Right then,' the superintendent said to the detectives. 'One of you remain here with this wet duck. Get the names of all the persons involved and the registration numbers of all the vehicles. Then transmit the details to the gardai manning the roadblocks. That way we'll capture them all.'

'Yes, sir,' the detective said.

'Come on,' the superintendent told the other detective. 'Let's go and get Pug Banzinni.' They hurried back to the car. The driver edged around the hearse and then put his foot down hard on the accelerator. The car shot forward.

'This is terrific,' the superintendent said to Cathy. 'Thanks to you and the boys, Pug Banzinni hasn't got away.' But Cathy couldn't speak. She was too overwhelmed by the praise.

The car quickly covered the distance to the cottage.

'This was their hideout,' Cathy said. The driver stopped the car by the gateway. But there was no sign of anyone. 'They may have gone on further,' Cathy added.

The superintendent spoke to the driver and he was

about to accelerate away when there was a whoop and three boys leaped up from behind the stone wall.

'It's them,' Cathy shouted. She didn't hesitate but opened the car door and leapt out. She ran towards the boys who had climbed over the wall and were racing towards her.

'We did it,' they shouted. 'We did it. We caught Pug Banzinni.'

When they had calmed down Cathy told them what had caused the delay. They in turn told her and the gardai all that had happened.

'We've got Pug Banzinni in the shed here,' David said, quite unable to keep the triumph out of his voice.

'Dobber and I brought him here,' Kevin said.

'Great work,' the superintendent said enthusiastically. 'Now we'll go and see if this Pug Banzinni is as frightening as they say.'

They all trooped towards the shed. Alan unlocked the door and Kevin reversed the cart out into the open. They stood for a moment looking at the coffin. Suddenly, from inside the coffin came a tapping noise. At this they all looked at each other and laughed.

'Right,' the superintendent said. 'Let's open it up.'

The detectives began to undo the brass screws on the lid. One by one they unscrewed them. When they were all undone, they lifted off the lid and stared into the box.

The effects of the paralysing drug had worn off and Pug Banzinni was able to rub his eyes with his knuckles. Then slowly he opened his eyes and blinked in the glare of the light. He stared up in puzzlement at the faces looking down at him.

'Where am I?' he demanded in a querulous voice. 'Am I on the trawler? I feel so seasick. Can't you stop this boat from rocking?'

'I'm afraid I can't,' the superintendent said, grinning.

'I demand to see the ship's captain,' Pug said. He stared up, glancing from face to face. 'Where's Speedy?' he asked. 'I want to see Speedy.'

'He's under arrest,' the superintendent said. 'And so are you, Pug Banzinni.'

'Banzinni?' Pug screwed up his eyes in puzzlement. But he couldn't quite hide his fear. 'I never heard of him,' he added. 'I'm Carlo Bonetti.'

'Oh no you're not,' Kevin said. 'You're Pug-nose Banzinni. That's a false beard and moustache you've got. See.' Kevin stepped forward and caught the end of Pug's false beard and gave a terrific tug. But Moran had used a very strong glue and the beard was stuck fast.

'Aahhh!' Pug bellowed in pain. 'I've been assaulted. Arrest him. Throw him in prison.'

'Be quiet,' the superintendent demanded in an authoritative voice. 'The only ones going to prison are you and your henchmen.'

'Oh no,' Pug Banzinni wailed now. 'This is all a terrible dream. I'll wake up soon and everything will be OK.' He looked as if he might cry.

'It's no dream,' the superintendent said. 'You're back at the cottage from where you set out. Thanks to these young people here, you didn't get away. Now I'm taking you into custody until another arrangement is made to fly you to America.'

At this Pug Banzinni suddenly sprang into a sitting position. His hand shot out and he grabbed Kevin's T-shirt. Before anyone could move, Kevin was dragged towards the coffin. His face was no more than inches from the ugly face of Pug Banzinni. The false beard tickled his nose and he felt Pug's hot breath on his cheek.

'I'll get you, boy,' Pug threatened. 'I'll have your hair pulled out strand by strand.'

But he got no further with his threats. To Kevin's relief, the detectives moved swiftly forward and caught Pug's arms. He was forced to release his grip and as he did so Kevin retreated.

The detectives pinioned Pug's arms behind his back and handcuffed him. Banzinni began to rant and rave.

Then he begged and pleaded, offering all sorts of rewards if he were allowed to go free. When this failed he began again to threaten them. But they all ignored him.

At that moment other gardai arrived in cars and on motorcycles. But they were too late. They stood around in a group while the superintendent told them what had happened.

'It's all thanks to these fine young people here,' he said, 'that this desperate criminal didn't get away.'

At this, Cathy and the boys blushed. It was embarrassing to be praised by such an important garda in front of all those others. But it was a good reason to feel proud too.

A garda approached just then.

'Excuse me, sir,' he said. 'We've just received a message on the radio that the helicopter has landed at Shannon Airport. The pilot and the decoy have been arrested. They're being taken to Limerick for questioning.'

'Very good,' the superintendent nodded, satisfied. 'Have you heard anything from the roadblocks yet?' he asked.

'No, sir,' the garda replied.

'Let me know the moment you do,' the superintendent said. 'Now, I must organise matters here.' He immediately detailed a number of gardai to take Pug

Banzinni to Swinford Garda station. Pug was helped out of the coffin and led away to a Garda car. He was shouting that he would take revenge on them all. The gardai bundled him into the Garda car and sped away with an escort of gardai on motorcycles with blue lights flashing.

'You had better be off home,' the superintendent told the Dolans and Alan, who had stood about while all this was happening.

'When you've told your parents of your adventures I want you all to come along to the station to make statements. The reporters will also want to interview you. This is a very big story. You will be on the television news tonight.'

They could hardly believe it. They would be seen on television by all the people they knew and by their school friends. It was fantastic.

'Off with you now,' the superintendent said. 'You've done a terrific job. We're all indebted to you.'

With the praise ringing in their ears, they set off. Kevin, Cathy and David drove off in the cart. Alan took his bicycle. Moonshiner's bicycle was left in the shed. David said he would get his father to return it and explain to Moonshiner exactly what had been happening.

Now David didn't take his bike to the bog that day. All four of them stayed together on the journey, each one relating his or her part in the adventure. They were anxious to get home and have the chance to relate the adventure all over again, to their parents this time.

As Pug Banzinni was being arrested, Slim and Tiny rendezvoused with Moran and the other thugs, as arranged. They transferred to one limousine and set off for Dublin. They were happy that things had gone so well, and were looking forward to the large rewards.

Joey was driving and it was he who first saw the roadblock up ahead. A Garda car was pulled across the road and a number of gardai were waiting. Joey slammed on the brakes and the thugs were jerked forward and then back like puppets.

'Something must've gone wrong,' Joey said in a fearful voice.

'Turn around,' Moran ordered. 'We can still get away.'

Joey nodded, and with shaking hands spun the wheel and pulled across the road. He then reversed, intending to do a three-point turn. But his nervousness made him careless. He went back much too far. There was a trench along the edge of the road and the rear wheels of the limousine dropped into it with a terrific jolt. Desperately Joey accelerated but the wheels spun wildly in empty space.

'Fool,' Moran roared, hitting Joey with his fists. 'You're

going to get us all caught. Come on. Out of the car. We'll have to push. Quickly now. The gardai are coming.'

The thugs glanced up the road towards where the gardai were piling into the Garda car. There was no time to lose. Prison awaited them all if they were caught. They scrambled from the car and rushed round to the rear. They got down into the trench and began to push with all their might.

Slowly the limousine inched forward towards the roadway. Just then the siren on the Garda car began to wail. As if it were a signal the thugs redoubled their efforts. A mighty push brought the rear wheels within inches of the edge of the trench. Another effort found the wheels on the grass.

As the wheels touched the grass Joey let out the clutch and pressed the accelerator to the floor. The wheels spun crazily and sprayed up grass and dirt and small stones right in the thugs' faces. Then the wheels gripped and the limousine shot across the road and hit the bank on the other side.

The thugs in the trench had thrown up their arms to try and protect their faces, but without success. Now, half blinded with the mud, they jostled and shoved each other. Tiny swung around in a last desperate effort to climb out of the trench. He knocked Moran over. Moran caught Slim's jacket and pulled him down with him. Bandy overbalanced and made a lunge for Tiny's legs to try and save himself. Tiny lashed out with one leg and he too lost his balance. He fell on top of the others, pinning them beneath him.

They were still struggling to untangle themselves and lashing out with fists and boots at each other when the gardai arrived on the scene. Within minutes they were under arrest and securely handcuffed. Their faces, all except Joey's, were black from the mud.

All the cars that came along the road slowed down to see what had happened. When the occupants saw the thugs they laughed and pointed at them. Children stuck out their tongues. One man took a photograph. The thugs fumed and swore but there was nothing they could do. When a Garda van eventually arrived to take them away they climbed into it without a murmur of dissent.

Once they were inside and the doors secured, the van sped away with an escort. The garda in charge picked up the radio mike and informed his superiors that the rest of the thugs were now on their way to prison.

# 22

# A TELEVISION APPEARANCE

That evening the Dolan family and Alan gathered round the television to watch the news. They were all excited at the prospect of seeing the details of that eventful day. The newscaster appeared and the item dealing with Pug Banzinni was first on.

'This afternoon,' the newscaster began in a grave voice, 'the aircraft taking the notorious criminal, Pug Banzinni, back to America was hijacked shortly after take off from Shannon Airport. The hijackers forced the plane to land at Knock Airport in County Mayo. It was there that a daring plan by Banzinni's henchmen to free him was thwarted by the brave efforts of three members of the local Dolan family and their cousin. Thanks to them Banzinni is right now on his way back to prison.'

At this the Dolans and Alan exchanged triumphant glances. They were famous.

'We are now going over to our reporter for details of the day's exciting events,' the newscaster added.

'This was the scene at Knock Airport this afternoon,' the reporter began, while the television showed pictures of the jumbo jet parked on the apron and taped off with yellow ribbon. Three uniformed gardai were guarding the aircraft.

'Two men hijacked this aircraft earlier today,' the reporter continued, 'and forced the pilot to fly it here to Knock. Once here the American criminal, Pug Banzinni, made a desperate but unsuccessful attempt to escape. I'm now going inside the terminal building to interview some of the persons involved in these events.'

There were pictures from inside the building with dozens of people and gardai milling about. The reporter interviewed Captain Mulligan and he explained how his aircraft was hijacked by Moran and Hal and how they used the threat to his daughter to force him to do as they said. He was fulsome in his praise of his crew and passengers and of the Dolans and Alan.

'I understand your daughter is now safe,' the reporter said.

'That's correct,' replied Captain Mulligan. 'When she

awoke in the late afternoon from her drugged sleep she found herself alone. By then she was suspicious and made her way to a nearby house. From there she phoned the gardai. All gardai in the Dublin area were informed of her abduction and, of course, they realised immediately who she was. She's on her way here from Dublin right now to join me.'

The reporter thanked Captain Mulligan and the superintendent was then interviewed. He explained who Pug Banzinni was and why he was in Ireland. He gave details of the trial and how the judge had decided to send Pug back to America. He then gave details of the elaborate plan which had been devised to free Banzinni.

'By now,' the superintendent said, 'we have arrested all the thugs who were involved in the plan. Acting on information received from them, we have arrested the couple who were at the house where Marian Mulligan was held and also the photographer who took the pictures. The captain of the Spanish trawler will also be dealt with in due course.'

'This was a daring plan,' the reporter said. 'How did it come to the notice of the gardai?'

At this, the superintendent hesitated. 'I must admit,' he said, 'that when it did come to our notice, Pug Banzinni had already escaped and indeed was on his way to freedom. I must say that if it wasn't for the bravery, intelligence and brilliant initiative of the young people you will soon meet at Swinford Garda station, the escape plan would have succeeded.'

At this point the screen faded out and then the reporter reappeared. 'I'm here now at Swinford,' he said, 'and I'm about to meet the young people whose efforts prevented Pug Banzinni from getting away.'

At that very moment David, Cathy, Kevin and Alan saw themselves appear before their eyes on the television. They listened to themselves give details of how they came to capture Pug Banzinni.

'It's certainly the most exciting story I've heard in a long time,' the reporter said. 'I must say you did show great bravery and initiative.'

The screen faded out again and the reporter reappeared.

'Those interviews were filmed earlier,' he said. 'But right now we are going over live by satellite to New York to interview the detective in charge of the case there.' There was a slight delay and then the head and shoulders of a man appeared on the screen.

'Captain Cooper?' the reporter asked. 'Can you hear me?'

'Sure, I hear ya,' the American replied.

'Well then, Captain Cooper,' the reporter went on,

'could you give me your reaction to what happened here in Ireland today?'

'Sure,' Cooper said. 'I'm mightily relieved, I can tell ya that. We've been after this Banzinni fella for a long time now. We thought we had him at last but it seems he nearly escaped from us again.'

'If it hadn't been for the intervention of the Dolans and their cousin he would have escaped,' the reporter pointed out.

'Yeah, I understand that,' Captain Cooper said. 'It was a very brave thing to do.'

'And do you have any message for them?' the reporter asked. 'I'm sure they're looking in right now.'

'I want to tell them,' Captain Cooper said, 'that the New York Police Department is very grateful for all they've done. They've prevented a most dangerous criminal from escaping and been responsible for the apprehension of his henchmen. In fact, we're so grateful that we would like them to come and visit us some time. We would love to have them here in New York.'

'Is that an invitation?' the reporter asked.

'Sure is,' Captain Cooper said. 'Soon as we've got Banzinni and his gang behind bars here we'll be writing to them young people inviting them to New York. All expenses paid, of course.'

'Are you inviting their parents too?' the reporter asked.

'Oh, sure,' Captain Cooper answered. 'Let them bring their grannies as well. We can manage them all.'

'Well, there you are,' the reporter said, turning to face the camera. 'If you're looking in, you lucky Dolans, you've just got yourselves a holiday in the Big Apple, granny and all. What do you think of that?'

At that moment, if the man had a camera in the Dolans' sitting room, he would have clearly seen what their reaction was to the good news. David, Cathy, Kevin and Alan were jumping up and down and whooping. Thomas and Mary Dolan were laughing and clapping their hands with delight. It was some time before they turned their attention back to the television. When they did so, the reporter was handing back to the studio.

The newscaster appeared.

'We are now going over to an outside camera,' he said. 'At just this moment Pug Banzinni is about to arrive back in prison.'

The television now showed a darkened street. In the distance could be seen vehicles approaching with blue lights flashing. There was a black van with steel grills over the windows. Garda motorcyclists and cars escorted it. The convoy sped along the street and swung in through a great gate. As the last vehicle entered the gateway, the gates clanged shut.

The camera swung away from the gate to a man with a microphone in his hand.

'Well, as we've just seen now,' this reporter said, 'the garda convoy bringing Pug Banzinni from Swinford Garda station has just arrived at the prison. Right now this desperate criminal is back behind bars. We can all sleep soundly in our beds tonight. Now, I'm handing you back to the studio for the rest of the news.'

'Well, that's it then,' Thomas Dolan said. 'All the excitement is over for today. Time to have supper and get off to bed. Heroes or not, there's still a lot of turf to be taken out of the bog.'

They all went into the kitchen where they ate their supper. But their excitement was still bubbling up. They discussed the prospective holiday and all the wonderful things they would see in New York.

They were still in the grip of excitement as they went off to bed. For a long time they all lay awake thinking of the exciting adventure they had had and of the holiday they had been promised.

Eventually sleep claimed them and they dreamed. In their dreams David and Alan were flying to New York. During the flight they were taken into the cockpit of the jumbo jet. Each had the opportunity to sit in the captain's seat and fly the plane. It was terribly exciting.

Cathy, too, dreamed that she was flying to New York. She was the most important person on the aircraft and was treated like a film star. All the passengers were talking about her and relating to each other how wonderful she was.

Only Kevin didn't dream of flying. Instead he dreamed that he was in a JCB. He sat in the driver's seat and worked the controls. He dug up great buckets of earth and filled them into lorries. It was, he decided the next morning, the most wonderful dream he had ever had.